SNATCHING *the* CATCHER

SNATCHING *the* CATCHER

Rebecca Connolly
Sophia Summers
Heather B. Moore

Mirror Press

Interior design by Cora Johnson
Edited by Kelsey Down and Lisa Shepherd
Cover design by Rachael Anderson
Cover image credit: Y-Boychenko, Deposit Photos #213065888
Published by Mirror Press, LLC

ISBN-13: 978-1-947152-62-5

Snatching the Catcher

Grizz is about to break all the rules for something
he never imagined he would be risking . . . his heart.

CHAPTER 1

"AND ONE . . . TWO . . . three . . . four . . . Breathe, and transition . . . two . . . three . . . four . . . You should all now be in extended triangle pose and breathing deeply . . ."

David McCarthy was most certainly not breathing deeply, and there was no way he was in any sort of triangle pose, extended or not.

He was a six-foot-four, two-hundred-and-sixty-pound man of all muscle and little else. He could throw a man out at second, from his knees and behind home plate, without breaking a sweat. He could throw out Levi Cox, which put him on a very short list of baseball players, let alone catchers. David could out-intimidate any hot-tempered batter in the league.

But he could not, in any way, form any sort of triangle pose like the class instructor was currently demonstrating.

He couldn't exactly see what pose he was making, but it felt more like a double Windsor.

Was that a yoga pose?

"Grizz! Grizz!"

He glanced over at his teammate Tiny, the motion making his neck hurt in ways he wasn't sure it was supposed to. "What?" he hissed.

Tiny, who looked like a freaking flamingo at the moment, grinned with all his Cuban charm. "How do you have yourself in a half nelson?"

David growled at him, which was a feat because, somehow, he actually did have an arm across his own neck.

"And transition again . . . this time to half moon," their breathy-toned teacher said as she miraculously tilted forward just enough to rest her palm on the floor and lift one leg without a hint of balance problems.

Yeah, right.

"Come on, Grizz," Tiny chuckled as he mirrored the teacher easily. "Half moon."

"I will kill you," David vowed, attempting to untangle himself.

Tiny shrugged and breathed with the rest of the class.

Breathed. Just because. While changing positions.

David shook his head and managed to get himself down into a plank, where he stayed and breathed, like a good student, and waited for something that didn't make him feel like an action figure being posed beyond the limits of his plastic design. He was not the sort of guy that could do yoga, and he was not ashamed of that. The others in the class were incredible with their abilities, strength, and flexibility, but he would never be among their ranks.

With some counselling, he should be able to accept that. Eventually.

He yawned without reservation, still breathing in his plank position, and looked over at a trim girl in a tie-dye tank top that could have been painted on her, her slender legs encased in black yoga pants. She was in a complicated position, without any trouble, and was eying him with interest.

Oh boy . . .

"It's all about the limits of your body!" she whispered, her eyes darting over to the teacher and back to him. "Mind over matter. You can do this!"

He blinked, wondering what she saw in him that made her think he was in any way capable of this class. "Thanks!" he whispered back, hoping she would ignore him.

She laughed and transitioned into a position that put her even closer to him.

Oh goody.

"Chad struggled at first too," she told him, indicating a guy across the room with her chin. "But look at him now!"

David looked and almost fell out of his plank pose.

The guy she was talking about was bigger than him in every way, built like a bodybuilder, and he was folding like a freaking pretzel.

That was unnatural.

"Such an inspiration," his attentive classmate said with a sigh. "He teaches a Mind, Body, Spirit class after this, if you want to stay."

"Can't," David grunted with as much of an apology as he could politely muster while moving into downward dog, quite possibly the only pose he actually knew and could almost do.

"Too bad," came the reply, her tone unquestionable as she held the pose absolutely perfectly.

David looked over at Tiny, who had heard the whole thing and was close to bursting with hysterical laughter.

"You are dead," David mouthed to the chipper shortstop.

Tiny didn't seem particularly concerned about the prospect.

Rookies. They never learned.

There were only a few minutes left in the class, which was a blessing. It hadn't been easy to accept the challenge from his coach to try a yoga class, especially when Tiny had said he knew of one and could go with him. Tiny wasn't one of his favorite teammates, but he wasn't one of his least favorites either. They were in the same boat, struggling to get their team to meet expectations after the roller coaster of last season.

No one had expected the Pittsburgh Knights to do anything, let alone clinch the wild card for the postseason. They'd even gone all the way to the World Series, though they had lost in four.

Easily.

After that, four of the seven biggest names on the team had traded out, and those that stayed were left scrambling.

David, or Grizz as everyone called him, was one of those guys, and he felt the pressure of it. But he also felt restless, ready for a change and for a team that would actually function as one.

He was one of the illustrious Six Pack, a group of six guys all drafted the same year from Belltown University, and every time one of the guys talked about how awesome their team was, he was jealous. Even Steal had a great team, and he was playing out in Minnesota for the Ice.

The Ice were a great team, but Steal hated the cold. No one felt bad for him, considering his success on that team, but still.

Skeeter had the Black Racers, and their season was lighting up already.

The others were in the mix too, but not David. Nope, the Knights were not going anywhere this year, and that meant the great Grizz wasn't either.

Not unless someone decided that being one of the Top Ten Hottest Pros counted as going somewhere.

He had to grin at that. The photo shoot had been absolutely ridiculous, and he had never felt more like a loser, including the time he had to wear a wrestling singlet and a bright-red wig while running the bases in Seattle after losing a bet to Axe Man. The Six Pack had, of course, loved when the magazine came out, not least because Big Dawg was in the Top Ten as well. Cole Hunter had, of course, ranked above David McCarthy in there, but ranks weren't important.

Or so David kept telling Big Dawg when it was brought up.

In truth, David didn't care about the Top Ten unless he was *with* Dawg or the others, and David's biological brothers gave him an even worse time about it than the Six Pack did.

It had been one of the very few times in recent history that he had shaved his token beard, and that, apparently, was the most shocking part of all. The beard was his in-season tradition, its growth having its own watch on TV, and it was probably one of his only protections against the world, stupid as that sounded. But he had dark hair, and the beard was even darker, and it grew full and thick, just as a Belltown Lumberjack alum would have wished.

It was how he'd gotten the name Grizz, actually.

A lifetime ago.

"And we breathe and come back to center," the instructor intoned as though she were talking them all off of a cliff, which was true for David. "Namaste."

The class recited it back to her, but David only snorted and moved for his shoes and bag.

"Feel renewed, Grizz?" Tiny asked as he followed, his eyes full of the sort of mischief David had come to expect from him.

David glared at his teammate as he sat and put his shoes on. "No."

"Oh well." Tiny tossed his shoes, tied together by their laces, around his neck and hefted his bag onto his shoulder. "See you at practice!"

"You're barefooted," David felt the need to point out as he rose again.

Tiny shrugged and wiggled his toes. "Reminds me of home."

"It's forty-five degrees outside."

"My car is at the curb."

David shook his head and waved his teammate away. "Crazy. Absolutely insane. Bye."

Tiny said something in Spanish as he left, and David only smiled placatingly at it.

He'd ask Axe Man about it later, and if it wasn't flattering, Tiny would pay tomorrow.

"Excuse me, but are you Grizz McCarthy?"

David turned with his ready smile, though it was a little harder to manage when he was irritated and sweaty for no good reason. "Yes, ma'am."

One of the women that had been in the front stood there, smiling at him with unmistakable interest. "I thought so. No one else could pull a beard off like that."

"I beg to differ, ma'am," David protested politely, sensing this was not an autograph opportunity. "I know several people who could."

The woman, who was at least forty years old, quirked her brows. "I don't." She took a step closer to him. "I saw that Top Ten issue of *Sports Monthly*, you know. You should have been number one."

David cleared his throat and kept his polite smile fixed as he grabbed his bag. "Have you seen Cole Hunter, ma'am? Take care." Before she could say another word or make another uncomfortable statement, he marched out of the room and headed directly for his truck.

"Stupid magazine," he muttered as he tossed his bag behind the seat and slammed the door. "Come on. Can't even have a yoga class in peace."

He paused as his truck roared to life, then took the liberty of slamming his head into the steering wheel to knock the idiotic statement out of his head.

On cue, his phone buzzed, and he made a face, letting the awkward vibrating continue in his pocket for a minute.

There was no way they could know.

No possible way.

His phone buzzed again, and he heaved a sigh, pulling the device out and glancing at the screen.

Rabbit: You guys hear about Grizz's new talent?

Skeeter: No . . . Tell me it's good.

Rabbit: Oh, I have pics.

David stared at the phone in horror. There was no way . . .

A picture of David's attempt at yoga appeared on the screen then, and it was even worse than he had imagined it could be.

Steal: Well, isn't that pretty?

Dawg: Such grace! Such poise!

Axe: I'm feeling rather zen at the moment.

David shook his head, laughing even as he felt a rare sense of embarrassment wash across his face. He responded the only way he knew how.

He sent a rather telling emoji.

Rabbit: Ooh, someone isn't feeling the zen.

Steal: Not enough namaste, bro?

Skeeter: Grizz, go meditate somewhere.

David rolled his eyes and responded, *I hate you all.* Then he tossed his phone onto the passenger seat and pulled out of his spot, driving away from the unremarkable strip of shops and boutiques in this random corner of Pittsburgh.

And this was how he was going to spend a late morning? Ridiculous.

He could have been sleeping in, not that he was very good at that anymore. He could have been having breakfast with

Hutch or Crocket, since they'd offered a dozen times, not that he was especially social with his teammates. He could have been at the gym, not that he needed any additional exercise.

He could have been with Rachel.

David's foot slipped off the gas pedal as he jerked at the thought, the truck awkwardly slowing with the sudden change.

"What the hell?" he muttered to himself, his face searing with heat as he adjusted his foot position and tried to resume driving like a normal human with a license.

He could *not* have been with Rachel. Absolutely not, and there was nothing that said he *should* be with Rachel at anything. For anything.

Ever.

Rachel Bennett was entirely off limits.

There was nothing in this world that could make it okay for him to be with Sis, of all people. Being Skeeter's little sister, she'd earned the name from almost the first day the Six Pack had formed at Belltown U, and her mother had been the resident mom to them all for the duration of their time there. It had been only natural for Rachel to become their sister in the same way, and there had been dozens of memories shared among them all.

Sis was family.

Except, after seeing her again at her mother's wedding last month, David found it harder and harder to think of her as Sis anymore.

She was Rachel now. Beautiful, funny, bright, vivacious Rachel—and a dance with her at the rehearsal dinner, and two at the reception, had only emphasized that image.

Staying out late with her the night before the wedding after the most rousing game of lumberball he'd ever played had given him more than one night of disgruntled indigestion.

Pleasant dreams, but resulting indigestion upon awakening, brought on by guilt.

Just because Rachel was in Pittsburgh too did not mean he had to do anything with her. Or call her. Or have any guilt about thinking about doing either of those things.

Guilt about calling a girl he'd known for years.

All because he couldn't get the image of her in the red dress from her mother's rehearsal dinner out of his mind.

"Easy, Grizz," he told himself as he pulled onto the interstate, letting his beloved Ram 2500 roar into action, blazing over the speed limit and not caring.

He needed the distraction.

Flipping his classic aviators down, David turned up his radio and began drumming out the beat on the steering wheel.

"Easy, buddy," he murmured again, ignoring the sign for the dance company Rachel happened to be with in Pittsburgh.

He had no reason to know or care about that.

Not a single one.

He turned his mind to other matters, actually important matters that would be a better use of his time.

Like figuring out how Tiny had snapped pictures *and* managed to send them to Rabbit.

And how he would make the twerp suffer for it.

Chapter 2

THIS WAS THE date that would never end.

Seriously, it was not going to end. The server had taken away their dinner plates at least twenty minutes ago, and Skyler had made it perfectly clear that he wasn't going to order dessert.

Something about his figure and caloric intake and not needing the added weight to his hips.

All of which he said while clearly indicating her own hips with his eyes.

She'd have thrown her fork like a javelin to his eye if they hadn't been in one of the classier restaurants in Pittsburgh, but Rachel Bennett had been raised to be respectful and polite and to represent herself well.

Stabbing one's date would be frowned upon.

So here she sat, twirling her fancy linen napkin around her fingers over and over in her lap, polite smile permanently fixed onto her lips, longing to escape before her dinner completely burned itself off and she was starving again.

She was going to kill Meghan for this. Rachel had a firmly established no-dating-dancers rule after the nightmare that

Kirk had been in her New York years, but Meghan had insisted that Skyler was amazing and that they would hit it off.

Rachel would like to hit *him* so this date would be off.

He was arrogant, spoiled, pretentious, and, if her instincts were correct, not nearly as good a dancer as he claimed. The names he'd dropped to impress her were people she'd done camps with over the years, and she'd managed to keep in contact with most of them. They'd never mentioned him, and dancers tended to talk about each other.

Rachel had heard of his company, of course, and it was more popular than hers, but popularity wasn't everything. She loved dancing with her company, Andante, and their programs were always challenging and beautiful. It wasn't big, it wasn't prestigious, but it was true to the art.

She wanted more, and she wasn't afraid to admit it, but she was also grateful to be dancing.

After failing in New York, she would always be grateful just to dance.

Skyler, on the other hand, was heading to New York to audition for two companies and a Broadway show next week.

Apparently.

She gave him a careful look, everything annoying her at the moment, from his ridiculously starched bow tie to the idiotic amount of product keeping his hair that towering and slick at the same time. Women all over the world would have killed for that volume, and he was managing it with ease. If he had any personality worth enjoying, she might have teased him about that.

As it was, he was droning on and on about doing a duet with LeeAnn Lyle three years ago at a workshop, which Rachel apparently ought to have been impressed by.

"She hasn't called me about joining her in LA," he was saying now as he slowly spun his glass of wine on the tablecloth, "but I have a call in with her agent. It's important to follow up on these things, you know."

"Mmm," Rachel replied, sipping her water.

"This has been nice," he suddenly interjected, dipping his voice into a lower octave and leaning forward in his seat, his eyes fixed on her.

Uh oh.

"Oh, good." Rachel forced a kinder smile. "Meghan was so hopeful."

"So am I."

Uh, no. Not happening.

Rachel began to scoot out of her seat. "It really has been nice meeting you, Skyler. Thank you for . . ."

Her forearm was suddenly seized and Skyler's look became predatory. "That's it? You think you can just have dinner with me and call it a night? We're not done."

"Seriously, Skyler?" Rachel gave him a disbelieving look and tried to wrench her arm away. "Let go."

He shook his head and smiled. "Not a chance. I've got plans for us tonight, and you won't be trying to get away then, I promise you. I can make you want it."

"Fat chance," Rachel spat, twisting her wrist to try and grip his arm with her nails, which happened to be decently long at the moment.

"Uh-uh," Skyler scolded as if this were all a game, holding her wrist in place. "Save that energy, kitten."

An indignant snarl was warming up within her, and flashbacks of her semester of self-defense roared to life in her mind.

How much trouble would she be in if she flipped the table on this piece of . . .

"Hey, Sis. I didn't know you'd be here tonight."

There was only one man in the world who could say

those words with a rumble that both tickled and terrified, and Rachel could barely keep from beaming at hearing it.

She didn't even look up at the towering man now standing beside her chair. "Hey, Grizz. Didn't I tell you?"

His hand fell on her shoulder, patting warmly, an unmistakable show of protection. "Nope, sure didn't." He squeezed very lightly, and her eyes began to burn. "Hi. Grizz McCarthy," he said, reaching out a hand to Skyler.

Skyler looked as though the jolly green giant had come to life, and he only blinked, then looked at Grizz's hand.

He'd have to let go of her arm to shake it.

Rachel saw him hesitate, then her arm was released, and he took Grizz's hand, trying for politeness. "Hi. Skyler . . ."

"Listen, Skyler," Grizz interrupted in his very congenial way, "I don't want to presume, and I certainly don't mean to interrupt, but I just saw you grab her arm, and from where I was sitting, it looked like you weren't going to let her leave."

Rachel bit her lip as she tucked her arm safely back into her lap, not ready to give up her seat to this show quite yet. Grizz still had Skyler's hand, and the skin of that poor hand was beginning to change colors.

"Now, if Sis here wants to leave," Grizz went on, the inflection of his voice not changing at all, "she gets to leave, am I right?"

Skyler swallowed, looking at his hand. "Well . . ."

"Because you really don't want to be that guy who disrespects women and treats them like property, right?"

Skyler's eyes widened, and Rachel would swear she heard him yelp. "I . . ."

"Of course not," Grizz overrode, patting Rachel's shoulder again.

She looked up at him, grinning freely, and he smiled down at her through the dark, somehow still neatly kept beard he wore. He winked, and she could have kissed the man for it.

Which made her cheeks heat.

What the . . . ?

He returned his attention to Skyler, his hand still in his grasp. "And now, my friend, conveniently, you don't even have to worry your overly coiffed head about getting her home. I'm here, so I'll just take care of that. You're welcome, pal."

"But . . ."

"She'll call you if she wants to go for round two," Grizz assured him, as if that were in any way likely. "But I'll be tracking her phone, as usual, so I'll know if you don't respect her boundaries. Bit overprotective, but you understand."

Skyler's face was white, and his attention was entirely focused on the slow death of his hand. "Uh . . ." he grunted.

Grizz leaned a little away and looked at Rachel, his brows rising. "I'm sorry, Sis, did you have anything to add? I'd hate to take over your date. Please, step in."

Rachel shook her head, smiling at Skyler. "Nope. I think you covered everything, Grizz."

"Thought so." Just then, his phone rang, the ringtone blaring out AC/DC in the relatively classy establishment. "Whoops, hang on, better get this."

He finally released Skyler's hand and pulled the phone out. "Grizz here. Hey, Big Dawg."

Oh, he didn't . . .

"Yeah, no, she's right here, hang on." Grizz pulled the phone away from his ear and put it on speaker. "It's for you, Sis."

Rachel could have died, but happily so. "Hello?"

"Hey there, darlin'!" Cole Hunter's gorgeous Texas twang greeted her from the phone. "You haven't called me in a while, so I thought I'd check with Grizz and make sure you were okay. You know how I worry about my gal."

Rachel nodded very soberly. "I do know. I'm sorry, love."

"Whatcha doin?" Cole asked. "Having dinner with Grizz?"

"No, actually," Rachel told him, smiling at Skyler, who suddenly looked ill. "I was having dinner with this guy named Skyler, a dancer friend of Meghan's. You remember her, right?"

"Sure, sure, great girl. You aren't dating behind my back, now, are you?"

"Cole," Rachel scolded him with another smile. "Of course not. You know how I feel about you."

"I sure do, darlin'. Hey, finish up with your friend's friend and call me tonight. I'm headed out to Tennessee with the team, but I always have time for you."

Oh, wow, Cole was really getting into this. She'd never hear the end of it now, and somehow, that was okay.

"You got it, love," she murmured, shaking her head. "Can't wait."

Grizz took the phone back, switching it off of speaker, and quickly said, "Right, that's enough. Getting awkward. Bye, Dawg."

Rachel took the opportunity to scoot out of her chair. "Sorry, Skyler. It really has been a memorable evening."

Skyler only nodded, keeping his eyes down.

Grizz gestured for Rachel to lead the way, giving her date a look. "You got the check, right, man?"

Without waiting for an answer, he put his hand on Rachel's back, and she started walking towards the coat check, her teeth digging into her lips.

Grizz didn't say a single word as they waited for their coats, as he helped her with hers and shrugged into his own.

It ought to be noted, she thought, that Grizz McCarthy looked rather fine in a leather jacket.

For the sake of observation, anyway.

Silently, he led her from the restaurant, and only when they were outside did she exhale, very slowly, her lungs shaking with the need to laugh.

Then Grizz let out a particularly loud snort, and Rachel lost it.

Laughter upon wave of laughter erupted from her, and she stumbled half blindly over to the raised planter near the outdoor seating of the now-closed cafe next door, sitting awkwardly. She covered her face as the laughter increased in volume and pitch, tears welling and overflowing without trouble.

"Oh," she gasped between giggles. "Oh my gosh." She pressed a hand to her chest, her breathing and laughing morphing into some awful faux hiccupping sound she couldn't control.

Somehow, through the haze of her laughter, she managed to get a glimpse at Grizz, who had collapsed to the ground and now sat against the planter box opposite, his head leaning back, his arms dangling over his knees, laughing freely.

Again, her cheeks heated, but she wasn't sure she minded so much.

"What in the world are you doing here, Grizz?" she asked, folding her arms and smiling with genuine fondness.

"Besides getting you out of a totally crappy date?" Grizz grinned cheekily, then sobered into his usual crooked smile. "I was having my usual dinner with my agent. Marcus is very fond of Italian, so this has become our go-to place every month. The chicken parm is especially good."

Rachel shook her head and tossed her blond hair in the cool night breeze, now smiling for no reason at all. "The chicken fettuccini was phenomenal tonight."

"Ooh, yeah, good stuff."

Something about his tone drew her attention, and she gave him a thorough look. "What?"

He raised his brows. "What what?"

"Tone, David," she replied. She waved a hand in encouragement. "Spill."

He laughed softly, the sound rippling up her spine. "Fine. What in the world were you doing with that?" He jerked his thumb towards the restaurant, leaving no doubt as to his point.

"Continuing my incredible streak," Rachel replied dryly, looking across the street at the park, lit up with strings of bulbs and white lights that gave it a romantic, nostalgic, completely classic feel. "I sure know how to pick 'em."

"You can't tell me you picked Skyler, the hope of all females."

Rachel snorted and covered her mouth, squeezing her eyes shut.

"That's what I thought."

"Stop," she protested, glancing over at him, loving the casual way he sat there, despite his nice slacks and button-up, though he was not wearing a tie.

It was an excellent look for him, that open collar.

She swallowed while staring at his throat. "No, I didn't pick Skyler, but I did break my cardinal rule of not dating dancers. Probably serves me right." She left out the unofficial vow she had made about not dating her brother's roommates, teammates, or friends.

That one was getting . . . hazy.

"No way," Grizz retorted, shifting his position to sit cross-legged, giving him a more intense look. "No way, Rach. That termite doesn't get a second thought from you, you hear me?"

Overprotective much?

Rachel pressed her tongue to the roof of her mouth, then smiled. "Hmm."

"Hmm?" he repeated, raising a dark brow. "What's 'hmm'?"

"You called me Rach," she pointed out, her smile feeling rather ticklish at the moment. "You always call me Sis."

Grizz returned her smile. "Not always. In there, it was easy. Call you Sis, he thinks you are. Out here, I can call you Rachel."

Yes, please!

She cleared her throat and sniffed in lieu of sighing or doing something equally pathetic over a guy she had once toilet papered Coach Maxwell's house with.

"Yeah, and you scared Skyler out of his mind," she covered with a laugh she faked more than felt. "And did you really have to get Cole involved?"

Grizz shrugged, the leather of his jacket crinkling against the brick. "I had to get someone to back me up. You would prefer that I called Skeeter? Let him be the brother he is, and I play boyfriend?"

The thought of her brother—her *real* brother—being involved made her queasy. "Sawyer can never know about that date, all right? I'll make you swear by Big Mack, if I have to."

"Whoa, whoa." Grizz held up his hands at the mention of the treasured Belltown Lumberjack, then glanced up at the sky with a wince. "Watch for falling Delilahs, will you?"

Rachel rolled her eyes, chuckling at the image of Big Mack's axe raining down. "Come on, swearing by the Belltown Lumberjack isn't going to make his axe fall from the sky."

He gave her a dark look. "You don't know that."

"Moron." She laughed once, then slapped the brick. "But seriously, Grizz. Cole?"

"He could be anyone's boyfriend at any given time, including on the spur of the moment." He shrugged again. "First guy I thought of. Sorry. Next time I'll choose Rabbit or Steal."

Rachel coughed and leaned her hands back against the planter box. "Oh, gosh, can you imagine?" She shook her head. "Thanks for that, by the way."

Grizz waved a dismissive hand. "Not a problem. I saw you earlier, and I thought about saying hi, maybe when I left or something. Then I saw you try to get up, and he grabbed your arm, and . . ." He held up his hands in a helpless gesture. "What can I say? I'm overprotective."

Woof.

"That's . . . that's really sweet, Grizz," Rachel murmured. "Thanks."

He smiled back at her. "It's not because you're Sis, you know."

Rachel's brows shot up. "Excuse me?"

"I mean, that's part of it," he admitted, rubbing his hands together almost absently. "I'd be lying if I said it wasn't, but . . ." His smile turned quizzical, almost confused. "I didn't come over because you're Skeeter's sister. Just cuz it's you."

Did he really have to make himself even more attractive right now? She was this close to fanning herself, and the night was not hot enough to write that off.

"I didn't mean to take you away from a meeting with your agent, Grizz," Rachel said quietly, not managing to sound nearly as apologetic as she should have been. "You can go back in; I'll get a car back to my place."

Grizz was silent, staring at her. "Rach, if you think I'd rather have dinner with Marcus than sit out here with you, you're insane."

There was nothing to say to that. She couldn't breathe, couldn't move, couldn't think . . .

Grizz? Really?

David freaking McCarthy . . .

"Well, I don't know Marcus," Rachel admitted wryly. "But I think I can safely say I'm a better date."

"Definitely," Grizz confirmed with a nod. "And you look a lot better too. That's a really great color for you."

Rachel glanced down at her outfit, something she'd had for over a year and had thrown on halfheartedly for this date tonight.

It was also all black.

She gave him an incredulous look. "Grizz, I'm wearing a black midi dress."

Grizz gave her a wide grin. "And black is a good color for you, Rach. So is red, as I recall."

Her face flamed at once, and she looked away, exhaling very slowly.

She'd worn red to her mother's wedding rehearsal dinner, and that night she had danced with Grizz and, for the first time, felt a flutter of excitement that was now a roaring tidal wave within her. They'd talked for hours that night, played lumberball with a bunch of others, met up for late-night donuts . . . And she'd been out later than any curfew she'd ever had in high school or college.

She didn't even have a curfew, but any time she was at home, it felt like she did.

Sawyer acted like she did.

It had been one of the best nights of her life, and nothing even remotely romantic had happened. With Grizz, of all people.

Who'd have thought?

"Well, in the interest of fair play," she managed to say, returning her attention to him, "that button-down with the open collar is a good look for you. So is leather."

Something changed in his expression, and it shifted something in the air between them. The night became somehow warmer and cooler at the same time, and all Rachel could do was smile at this man she had known for years but somehow never really seen until this very moment. This man who had made her laugh, but never made her cry; had teased her, but never hurt her; had hugged her, but never held her.

That was one thing she desperately wanted to change.

"So," she added, forcing lightness into her tone, "the Knights playing at home this weekend?"

Grizz nodded slowly. "We are. You interested in coming?"

Was she ever.

But no, she had to play this cool.

She lifted a shoulder. "Maybe. Know a guy who can get me good seats for cheap?"

"As a matter of fact, I do," he replied, his tone matching hers. "I'll give him a call tomorrow and let you know."

"You'll put me on a list or something?"

He slowly shook his head. "Nope. I'm gonna make you earn them."

"What?" she protested with a laugh. "Grizz, come on!"

"Hey, I don't ask for favors in your occupation," he insisted as he got to his feet and brushed off his pants.

Rachel scoffed loudly. "What, you want tickets to see Andante in concert?"

"I'd love some, actually."

Her budding laughter and doubt vanished into thin air. "Wait, what?"

Grizz shrugged, clearly his favorite bodily motion. "Why not? You've seen us all play, but we've never seen you perform. *I've* never seen you perform, and I'd like to."

Rachel wet her lips. "Seriously? Sawyer never told you horror stories of watching my recitals and shows?"

"I make it a point to never listen to anything Skeet says off the diamond," Grizz informed her in a deadly serious tone that made her grin without shame.

"That may be the best thing I have ever heard," she admitted, with a faint laugh.

Grizz smiled back. "But that isn't how I want you to earn them. How about breakfast Saturday morning?"

Rachel leaned back, surprised, to say the least. "Don't you have a team breakfast or something?"

"Nope. We're pros now. We sleep in, and our fancy housekeepers and chefs keep us well fed." He rocked on his heels a little, and it was an adorable if amusing sight.

"Uh-huh," she murmured. "So is your chef making this breakfast on Saturday that I may or may not attend?"

He made a face and snapped his fingers. "You know, I think I gave her the weekend off. We'll have to settle for Eddie's."

Now she was blown away. "Eddie's? On Bakersfield?"

Grizz's expression matched hers. "You know it?"

"It's four blocks from my apartment," she breathed, eyes wide. "I go there every Sunday."

"I'm there on Saturdays when I'm in town," he told her.

They had regularly been within walking distance of each other in this massive city, and they had never known it? They'd never looked into it? Never figured that out?

How had she missed that?

"Well," Grizz said in a very low voice, "now you have to meet me there. It's fate."

He was teasing, but she couldn't laugh.

Was it really fate?

She was afraid to find out.

And curious enough to risk it. "Okay," she whispered, her lips curving of their own accord. "Saturday at Eddie's. Nine o'clock okay?"

"Perfect."

They stood there for a number of heartbeats, just staring at each other, charged with anticipation or excitement or nerves, or maybe a combination of them all.

Rachel, for one, was this close to giddy.

Over David flipping McCarthy.

Lord have mercy.

"Come on," Grizz finally said, exhaling in a telling gust of air. "I'll take you home." He nudged his head down the street and offered her an arm, keeping his hand in the pockets of his jacket.

Feeling amused and a little coy, Rachel came over and looped her arm loosely through his. "That would be nice, Grizz. And I know a great ice cream place on the way."

"Awesome. I could use a milkshake."

"Me too."

Chapter 3

"Come on, Grizz, here we go, baby, here we go now!"

David craned his neck from side to side, clapped his arms across his chest three times, then raised his bat up to look at the tip as he stepped towards the plate. He eyed the catcher and nodded once. "Hey, Gates."

Through the mask, Gates grinned up at him. "Sup, Grizzy? Gotta get that growth goin', man."

David jutted his chin out pointedly. "Still early in the season, bro. Don't hate. You'll get a few whiskers soon, I'm sure of it."

"Shut up," came the laughing reply.

Turning his attention to the pitcher, David sobered and readied himself at the plate. This guy was a rookie, but his arm was ridiculous. Unpredictable at best and wild at worst. David had been studying the kid for a few weeks, and he was impressive, to say the least.

Could he hit off him, was the question.

The kid wound up and released, and David swung, wincing mentally as he felt nothing but air in the swing.

"Strike!"

David exhaled and stepped back just enough to reset.

"Come on, Grizzy, get me there!" AD called from third.

"Grizzy, get him, kid!" someone shouted from the dugout.

Another slow exhale, and he hovered in his position, waiting.

The pitcher shook his head once, twice, then a nod. He came set.

The ball was released, and it was a beautiful, perfect pitch.

Right where David wanted it.

He swung the bat and connected right in the sweet spot he loved. He took off for first as the ball soared and dropped perfectly in the corner of left field. That would get AD home and get a good position for Hutch with only one out. David reached second base easily and stopped there, nodding to Lee, the coach on third, who indicated he stay there.

Job done.

He exhaled and wiped off his gloves, grinning over at the dugout, where his teammates were imitating a touchdown celebration dance.

Idiots.

"Hey, Grizz," the second baseman greeted as he came to stand near him.

David glanced at him, still smiling. "Hey, Birdman. How are you liking DC?"

Birdman shrugged and scratched at his baby scruff. "Not bad. Fans are great. Still trying to fight the good fight, you know?"

"I do know. Well, your numbers are good, so keep it up, huh?"

Birdman smiled and tapped him with his empty mitt. "Thanks, Grizz."

David tapped the brim of his helmet in acknowledgement, then focused on the batting at hand.

Hutch homered on the third pitch, driving them both home, and David was grateful for the opportunity to sit and breathe for a moment before he had to get back out there. He picked up a cup of water from the top of the bench behind him and sipped slowly.

"Hey, Grizz! You got that ball's number, huh?" Tiny crowed loudly as he came over, slapping the bench next to David enthusiastically.

"Go away," David grunted as he kept his eyes on the field.

"Ooh, somebody's not having a good day," his teammate said.

David flicked his eyes to Tiny. "You sent pictures of that stupid class to Rabbit. You know I only went because Lee bet me I wouldn't."

Tiny grinned with all the mischief David had learned to accept from his teammate. "Couldn't resist, man."

David stared at Tiny, then whistled once.

On cue, Hutch and Lima rose from their seats, each taking one of Tiny's arms and carrying him to the cooler of water on the ground. They turned him upside down, with the help of AD and Bert, and dunked his head in the water.

"Come on!" Tiny yelled as the entire dugout laughed. "Man, that's the drinking water!"

David looked down the line of his teammates. "Anybody upset?"

"No!" came the chorus of guys.

Tiny was righted, and the others went back to their seats to cheer on the others.

"Thanks, boys," David said as he tossed some sunflower seeds into his mouth.

Tiny shook his head like a dog, water spraying everywhere. "Oof. That was brisk, Grizz. Not nice."

David shrugged. "Neither is sending an embarrassing photo of me to the Six Pack. We're even."

Cowboy was tagged out after T-Money hit a pop fly to second, and the Knights rose almost as one from their positions on the bench, mitts in hand.

Reaching for his shin guards and knee savers, David groaned and shrugged into his chest protector before getting up and leaving the dugout. He grabbed his mask and helmet from the dugout fence and moved towards the diamond, whistling to himself.

"What has you in such a fine mood, Grizz?" Sherlock asked with a swat to David's back. "We're still down a run."

"Yeah," David admitted, looking over at the youngest pitcher on the team, "but it's a beautiful day, and we're playing baseball."

Sherlock gave him a bewildered look. "We play baseball every day. And the Rebs shouldn't be beating us."

David crouched just outside the dirt and put his shin guards and knee savers on with efficient, habitual motions. "Come on, you know the Rebels are worth a shot. And we've got time; it's only the sixth. Don't worry about the numbers. We're just playing baseball. You just get out there and do your thing. One more inning, Sherlock, and it's got your name all over it."

Sherlock nodded and headed out to the mound.

"Ladies and gentlemen, returning to the mound, starting pitcher, Andrew Holmes!"

David chuckled and put on his helmet and mask, shaking out his legs, then sinking down into his position. He glanced back at the umpire, who nodded at him.

He grinned back.

It didn't hurt to be friendly with the umps, really.

The first batter came to the plate, and David knew this guy was a hothead. He'd pick a fight with his own teammate if the mood was right, and any perceived attack would set him off.

He'd already been struck out twice, so he wasn't exactly chipper.

David signaled to Sherlock and received the nod in return.

Keep it clean, man. No questions.

The first pitch was a beauty, right down the middle, nothing anyone could dispute.

David nodded to Sherlock as he threw the ball back to him, then signaled for another.

Come on, get him out.

Sherlock shook his head.

David signaled another.

No.

One more time.

Yes.

David shifted for the curve, not happy with the decision. Sherlock's curve balls were unreliable, and with this guy at bat . . .

Sure enough, the ball whizzed right by the batter, but only by the skin of his teeth. The batter jumped back and glared at Sherlock, pointing the bat out towards him like a sword. "I'm giving you just one!" he yelled to Sherlock. "Don't mess with me!"

"Hey, hey, hey," David said from his position, tossing the ball back. "Cool off, man. Come on, let's play ball. Let's go."

The batter looked directly at David. "Tell your boy to mind his pitch, you hear me?"

David cocked his head at the guy but kept his mouth shut.

He didn't take kindly to being ordered like that.

At all.

David punched his glove and tipped his chin, looking back towards the mound. He signaled the pitch, and was surprised that he got a nod so fast.

What was Sherlock up to?

As soon as he released the ball, it was clear what he was doing.

The ball hit the batter in the upper arm, and almost at the same moment, the bat was dropped. The batter charged the mound in long, furious strides.

David tossed his mask off and dashed after him. "Whoa, whoa, whoa . . ."

Sherlock dropped his glove as the batter approached, and he ducked as a punch was thrown at him. The infield swarmed, and the dugouts cleared as players raced to avenge their teammates.

This was ridiculous, but it came with the territory, and David had learned how to handle things.

"No!" he barked, shoving Tiny away. "Get back, get out."

David shrugged off the arms of a player on the Rebels, and headed straight for Sherlock and his attacker, both of whom were still at it. "Sherlock, knock it off!" He ducked as a swing came in his direction, and he came up behind Sherlock, wrapping his arms around him and hauling him away.

He glanced over his shoulder. "Gates, get your guy out of here!"

The Rebels' catcher mirrored David's hold on his guy, and before long the key players had been removed from the fight, leaving the rest to deal with the fallout.

"What is wrong with you, Sherlock?" David snapped in his pitcher's ear. "What was that?"

"So my pitch went wild," came the irritated reply. "So what? He deserved it."

David snorted in response. "Cheap shot, cheap excuse. Cool off over there."

"You're not the coach!"

"No, but he thinks like one," Coach Barker said as he approached them, shaking his head. "Sherlock, you're out."

Sherlock jerked out of David's hold. "What? Come on, Coach, he charged me!"

Coach nodded once. "He did. And you're out. Take a seat."

Sherlock glared, his jaw working. Then he shook his head and marched into the dugout, skipping the benches and moving straight into the clubhouse.

Coach looked over at the bullpen and signaled for a right-handed pitcher, then turned to David with a heavy sigh. "Having fun, Grizz?"

"Loads," David deadpanned. He looked over the bullpen and smiled slightly at the approaching relieving pitcher. "Ah, Barney. Good. Should put this away nicely."

"Here's hoping," Coach grumbled as he watched the field clear. "Give him three, Grizzy, and end this."

David nodded. "Yes, sir." He waited for Barney to reach him, then swatted him on the backside. "Here we go, Barney. Give me three, and let's go."

Barney, one of the more experienced pitchers, grinned easily. "Heave-ho, right?"

David held up a warning finger. "Don't do that. Only Lumberjacks get that right."

"Fine," Barney retorted as he punched his glove lightly. "Then here's mine: hoo-rah!"

"Semper fi, my man," David replied, nudging his arm. "Let's go." He jogged back to home plate and looked up at the stands behind it, doing a quick scan.

No Rachel.

Good.

This was not the game he wanted her to see. The Knights were not their best right now, and with that fight, feelings would be running high, and not in a good way. His team was disorganized enough; they didn't need any help being distracted and losing focus.

When Rachel came to see him play, it needed to be a clean game. A team they could beat.

He needed to impress her.

A woman who had spent a lifetime attending baseball games. That seemed strange.

And yet not strange.

Not strange at all.

He shook his head and picked up his mask and helmet, putting them on quickly. He'd said no distractions for the team, and here he was.

Distracted.

By thoughts of Rachel Bennett.

"You all right, Grizz?" the ump asked as he chomped on his gum.

Right. Baseball. Three warm-up pitches, then game on.

Right.

David nodded, flashing a quick smile, and sank down, opening his glove for Barney's pitches.

Baseball first, then Rachel.

Hopefully.

"Whoa, girl. What are you saying?"

Rachel rolled her eyes and settled into the couch more. "I'm saying I'm having breakfast with a family friend tomorrow, that's it."

Meghan sat up, straw still hanging out of her mouth, her messy bun somehow messier now as the chocolate strands of her hair dangled around her face. "Family friend. Grizz McCarthy. Grizz 'my future husband' McCarthy."

"Well, I don't know about that," Rachel laughed, tossing a pillow at her friend. "He played baseball with my brother, we went out with the old group during my mom's wedding weekend. We're both in Pittsburgh, and when we ran into each other during my date the other day . . ."

Meghan hissed a wince. "I am so sorry about that date. I had no idea Skyler was such a creep now."

Rachel waved that off. "Whatever, it's done. Anyway, we're getting breakfast at Eddie's to catch up. That's it, end of story."

"Or beginning of story," Meghan said in a deeply suggestive tone.

"Stop." Rachel shook her head and drew her knee to her chest. "It's just Grizz."

"'Just Grizz?'" Meghan repeated, dark eyes wide. She snorted once. "Hon, didn't you see the Top Ten in *Sports Monthly*? Two of your blessed Six Pack made it, and the pictures are all kinds of hot."

Rachel shook her head. "Nope. Nope, not gonna. These guys are practically my brothers, Megs."

Meghan gave her the sort of look a person gives someone wearing shorts in a blizzard. She held up a finger, got up, and went to her bag, pulling out the magazine in question. She tossed it to Rachel, and it landed in her lap.

"What did I say?" Rachel insisted with a laugh.

"Look at it," Meghan insisted. "I'm going into the kitchen for ice cream, and when I get back, I'll hand you the pint you'll need after looking." She gave her a knowing look, then left the room.

Rachel glanced down at the magazine, some football player on the cover, his shirt off, looking ripped and staring the camera down.

"Do I really need this version of them in my head?" Rachel murmured to herself.

Cole, she most certainly didn't. She knew what a playboy

he was, though he was the biggest, sweetest softie in the world under his Texas charm. He put on a show, but he was one of the good guys, for sure. It wouldn't change her perception of him at all to see him showing off for the camera.

Grizz, on the other hand . . .

Grizz was the kind of guy who instantly made you comfortable. He was a tough guy in looks, but in every other respect, completely the opposite. Granted, he could intimidate the heck out of anybody, and she'd seen him stand up to a mouthy batter back in college. The guy had cowered like a puppy just by looking at the towering Grizz.

Rachel had never seen Grizz as scary. Not for a moment. She couldn't.

But hot? A Top Ten hottest professional athlete?

The magazine was flipped open before she could think another thought.

She skimmed over the other athletes without hesitation, not particularly caring about the hockey stars, football boys, or anyone else. A brief snort of amusement escaped when she saw Cole, but it was a fleeting glance she gave him at best.

Her heart stopped when she saw it.

Grizz was shirtless, just like everyone else had been, and he was clean-shaven, which was a sight very few people saw. He wore jeans, had his catcher's mask pushed back on his head, and held a baseball bat over one shoulder. The black paw tattoo on his upper arm added a more intimidating, gritty side to him, something primal and raw.

Beyond that, she really couldn't think.

His eyes were a shade of blue she was positive she had never seen in real life, and they bored into her with the same effect jumping into an icy lake had. Her lungs seized up, her head swam, and her limbs went numb.

That build . . .

That smirk . . .

That . . . That . . .

That was most definitely not the Grizz McCarthy she knew. Or, if it was, what the *heck* was wrong with her?

Grizz had never made her drool in her entire life. Or feel incredibly warm. Or suddenly want as much ice water as humanly possible. Yet here she was, fully salivating, flushed, and thirstier than she could ever remember being.

Grizz McCarthy was a sexy man.

Like the sexiest.

She'd always given that title to Cole, not out of personal attraction but simply a natural point of fact.

At this moment, her overheated feminine brain was asking the question, "Cole who?"

And Grizz was the man she had agreed to have pancakes with in the morning?

He could have fried her eggs on his twelve-pack abs, sizzled bacon on his chiseled chin, and drizzled syrup over every blessed nook and crevice, and she'd have thanked him for letting her watch. And she had the strangest desire to press her hand against that paw tattoo, then dig her fingers into that blessed muscle and hold on for dear life.

There was no way to unsee this.

No freaking way.

She swallowed what felt like a dozen marbles and fanned herself with one hand, eyes wide.

Tomorrow would be a breakfast of water and eye candy with a side of parched throat.

Heaven help her.

Something cold touched her right cheek, and blindly she reached for the pint, her eyes staying trained on Grizz.

A spoon was placed in her other hand.

"Eat up, girl," Meghan teased, her voice sounding fuzzy somehow. "You're gonna need it."

Rachel nodded absently, flicked the lid of the ice cream off, and dug out a huge spoonful that she proceeded to shove into her mouth.

She couldn't even taste the flavor.

Chapter 4

His palms were sweating.

He couldn't remember the last time that had happened, and he'd played in the World Series last year.

Baseball was easy.

This . . . this was terrifying.

But here David sat, by himself, at his usual table at Eddie's, close to drumming his fingers on the surface of the table.

It felt like Rachel was late. She wasn't; his watch and the clock on the wall both showed that she had ten minutes before the time they had settled on. But he'd been here long enough to guzzle two glasses of water, scan the menu three times, and check his watch twenty-four times.

Waiting sucked.

The bell above the door chimed, and David found himself perking up like a puppy for a tennis ball, hoping . . .

Dark sunglasses were pushed back over a blond bob, and hazel eyes searched the diner while slender, toned arms brushed at a simple gray T-shirt.

Rachel.

Her eyes clashed with his, and she smiled, perfect curve and flash of white teeth socking him in the gut with more force than any of the guys had ever done.

He exhaled and belatedly rose, remembering to smile himself as Rachel wove through the tables towards him.

"Hi," he greeted her, his wit astounding himself, clearly showing his impressive intellect to his date.

Date? This wasn't a date, it was breakfast. It was just Sis, and they were catching up.

"Hey," Rachel replied, sliding her hands into the pockets of her jeans as she grinned up at him.

Mental tires squealed in his brain, and for some reason, he laughed to himself.

"What?" Rachel demanded when he did.

He shrugged, mirroring her pose, his hands going to his pockets. "It's good to see you, and this is totally awkward."

Her eyes widened meaningfully, her grin spreading. "Totally. I've heard pancakes are good for that."

"Biscuits and gravy too." David gestured to the chair across from him. "This okay? It's my regular table, but if you want somewhere else . . ."

"Psht," Rachel scoffed, taking the seat and crossing her legs. "I am not that particular, Grizz." She eyed the glass of water and raised a brow at him. "Please tell me you aren't on a strictly water kick. Sawyer did that once, and it was so annoying."

David chuckled and took his seat. "Water before food, chocolate milk during food."

Rachel raised her hand for a high five, and he responded accordingly, though it made him feel like this was just breakfast with a friend.

Which was exactly what it was, but he wanted something else.

Something more.

Clearing his throat, he pulled the menu open again. "Anyway . . . Saturday specials are pretty good, I hear. Johnny over there was saying . . ."

"David . . ."

He hated that name. Not really, but he almost never was called that. His nieces and nephews called him Uncle Grizz, his brothers called him all sorts of things, and his mother called him Davey, for some reason no one understood.

But this time, it made him smile.

He peered over the top of the menu. "Rachel Grace . . ."

"Oh, no," she retorted with a very firm shake of her head she had obviously learned from Mamma Sal. "Nope. Full-name usage not okay."

"You called me David," he pointed out. "Fair is fair."

She made a face. "I didn't use your middle name."

"You don't know my middle name."

"Still."

David chewed his lip, pretending to think, then he sighed. "Fine, fine, you win. It's Edward, okay?"

Rachel's brow furrowed, and her lips formed a quizzical almost smile. "I don't remember . . ." Then she switched gears and nodded very sagely. "Excellent, I will store that away for future reference. Edward, your father's name. Good choice." She laughed and cocked her head at him. "Why didn't the older brothers get it?"

"Easy," David replied as he flagged down the waiter. "Tony got Grandpa Joe's name, Mike got Grandpa Pete. I got Dad, and Clint . . . Poor guy got Mom's maiden name."

He watched Rachel's lips spread back into a smile. "Which is . . . ?"

"Harper."

"That's not bad."

"Layman," he continued. "Harper-Layman. My brother's name is Clint Harper-Layman McCarthy."

Rachel clamped down on her lips hard, a beautiful giggle struggling to erupt against the obstructions as the waiter set down a glass of water for her.

"Yep," David confirmed, though she hadn't said anything. "My brother is the world's classiest law firm of a name."

She made a face at that. "Technically, my brother is one too."

David hadn't thought of that. Sawyer Charles Bennett.

Yep, that worked.

David raised his glass in the air. "To law-firm brothers."

Rachel somberly raised her glass and clinked it against his. "Poor souls." She looked at their teenage waiter as he walked up to the table. "We're both going to need chocolate milk, Paul. With at least one refill each."

"And a plate of biscuits," David added.

"And gravy."

Paul nodded, jotting it down. "Right away. And your meals?"

"Hmmm." Rachel pursed her lips, then clicked her tongue once. "Paul, can I convince you to give me banana *and* strawberry with the Nutella crepes?"

"Sure," the kid said right away. "Any sides?"

Rachel folded the menu and handed it to him. "Hash browns, please."

David shook his head. "Weirdo."

"Excuse you," Rachel shot back, kicking him under the table. "Your opinion on my breakfast is not required. Your turn."

He didn't bother fighting the smile. That kick did crazy things to him and, oddly enough, immediately put him at ease.

"Cowboy omelet," he told Paul, keeping his eyes on Rachel. "Side of bacon, if you don't mind, and make it crispy."

"Just like usual, Grizz, you got it," Paul said as he wrote it all down. He tucked the pencil behind his ear and nodded as he headed off to the kitchens.

Rachel snickered as she uncrossed her legs, sitting up to sip her water. "The usual. You have a usual."

David grinned. "I'm willing to bet you do too."

Her mouth dropped open to protest it, then instead she laughed. "Guilty," she admitted. "Strawberry-and-chocolate-chip pancakes."

"I didn't see that on the menu."

"It's not," came the unapologetic reply. "I ask nicely."

That would do it.

He wouldn't tell her that would work for him too, but it was an interesting thought to hang onto.

"How does a woman who eats strawberry-and-chocolate-chip pancakes and strawberry-banana-Nutella crepes not gain a thing?" David asked with a shake of his head. "It's just not fair."

Rachel held her hands in a dramatic shrug. "I dance, Grizz. And you should talk. You don't have a spare ounce."

Wait, what?

Had she checked him out?

How had he missed that fascinating insight?

Then it dawned on him.

He slumped back into his chair, shaking his head repeatedly. "You saw it."

"I sure did," she responded, sounding amused. Her hazel eyes danced with a new light as she looked at him. "Quite an interesting read."

Read? The thing was five paragraphs of "About Me" questions he'd had to answer, and none of them were particularly enlightening. Marcus had made him do it, said it would be good for his image, but it was a stupid gimmick. Big Dawg was the flashy one, not David.

He shook his head again. "I'd like to burn every copy of that issue. Never felt more like a sideshow in my life."

"I don't think the magazine needs any more heat than it already has in it," Rachel mused, spinning her glass of water slowly on the table. "Like I said, interesting read."

David perked up, his ears burning with sudden warmth. "Oh yeah?" he murmured slowly. "How interesting?"

She lifted a slender shoulder in a decent attempt of a shrug, her eyes still on him, that glass still turning. "Enough. Someone could make posters out of those pictures, put them on the wall."

There was something incredibly attractive about this playful banter she was tossing out, and he felt like he could grin for years. "Which ones would go on your wall, Rachel Bennett?"

The glass stopped turning. "Well, I have to put my boyfriend, Cole, on there, or he'll get crazy jealous."

David coughed a laugh of surprise but humored her by nodding. "Yep. Can't upset him. Anyone else?"

"That guy who plays running back for the Wolves is pretty good-looking . . ."

"Nah," David scoffed as Paul returned with their chocolate milk. "He's not as tall as he looks. Totally distorted."

Rachel snapped her fingers in apparent disappointment. "And I was so hopeful. Well, guess I'll have to go with what's already up on the wall."

"Already?" he repeated with interest. "Do tell."

She gave him a slow, smoldering smile. "A girl needs her secrets, David."

His name again.

Why?

"You keep calling me that," he brought up as he opened the straw and dropped it in his glass. "Got a point?"

Rachel shifted in her seat, her eyes dropping away for the first time, her hands going to her lap, her shoulders hunching.

Was she uncomfortable? She'd been so confident, so natural before, but could she possibly have been feeling the same crawling tension he was?

"Rach?"

She shifted again. "Full disclosure?" she asked, still looking small in her chair.

His stomach dropped. "Of course."

Her hazel eyes hit him again. "I wanted to know if it was different to call you David instead of Grizz." She paused a beat. "It's not. You're still you."

David stared at her, his pulse pounding furiously in his ears.

Rachel Bennett was a gorgeous woman, funny and bright, athletic and graceful, and she knew him.

She *knew* him.

"Wow," he breathed.

Rachel's brows lifted. "Wow what?"

He shook his head, smiling crookedly. "Just wow."

She returned his smile with a wide one of her own. "That's not much to go on, Grizz."

"David," he told her gently, lifting his glass of chocolate milk just a little.

She lifted hers to clink against his. "Whatever you say."

"No, Rach. Whatever *you* say."

"Ugh," Rachel groaned, though her cheeks began to glow a bright pink. "Don't be charming. I'm already having trouble looking at you after that magazine."

She was *what?*

"Really?" he asked, sounding far more eager than he'd meant to. That was supposed to be a calm, collected, very Cole Hunter drawl of confident pleasure.

Not a six-year-old who gets told he can have a kids' meal at his favorite drive-thru.

Rachel propped her elbows on the table, covering her face with her hands. "Are you really doing this?"

"Doing what?" He laughed and spread his hands out. "It's just a question, Rach."

She dropped her hands and gave him a very thorough look. "David, don't you know how ridiculously good-looking you are?"

The breath in his lungs evaporated. "I . . ."

Rachel tilted her head. "There's no good way to answer that, is there? Fine. Don't. Suffice it to say, you are an exceptionally good-looking man, not that any particular magazine needed to tell me that, and certain recent photos of you put a very large, very intense exclamation point on the darn thing." She cleared her throat and sat back, waving her hand absently. "Change the subject. Now, please."

Aside from wanting to tell her how beautiful she was, and how he never wanted to leave this diner, he wasn't sure where to take the conversation.

All he knew was that he couldn't stop smiling.

"How's work?" he started, the words feeling even lamer than he sounded, but he still smiled.

"We're going back to basics, huh?" Rachel chuckled and sipped her chocolate milk. "Love it. Okay, work. Not so much love. Way too much drama for a dentist office. People have no idea, but adults aren't any more mature than junior high girls. Drives me bonkers."

David shook his head, puzzled. "Then why work there? You're an administrative assistant, right?"

She wrinkled up her nose. "Kind of, but not really. I work front desk. Three-quarter time so I can still dance, but enough to get me benefits." Her lips curved in an ironic smirk.

"There's no money in dance. I tried. Gotta pay the bills to follow my dreams."

He nodded in understanding. He had been lucky, drafted right out of college and a full-ride scholarship during, but his brothers had careers they'd had to fight for. Clint was a Marine, and David had heard all about his training, every gritty detail. Tony and Mike were in finance, but he'd never been able to differentiate between their particular positions, no matter how many times they'd explained it.

"Still," he said. "You deserve a day job that doesn't irritate you."

Rachel shrugged once. "Drama comes with working with women. I can deal. I'm outside the clique, so I just do my job and leave when the clock says to. Then I get to dance."

David laughed softly to himself and didn't wait for her to question it. "Did you know that your voice goes soft when you say the word dance?"

"No," Rachel admitted with a shy smile. "But it makes sense. It's my passion. I wasn't a dance major because nothing else fit. Didn't matter that we couldn't afford to send me to a fancy dance school or that I had to make do with dancing just on the high school teams. I just wanted to dance. It was all I ever wanted to do."

"I know. I remember."

Rachel looked startled for a moment, then tossed her head back on a laugh, her throat dancing with it. "Oh, lands, I forgot. Sawyer made you all come over and talk to me about college. Thought I wouldn't make anything of myself if I majored in dance."

David nodded and folded his arms on the table top. "Send in the Brothers Six Pack. And all we did was make you more determined."

Rachel matched his position. "Dang straight. I wanted to

dance for the rest of my life, and none of you were going to change my mind."

"We told Skeet that," he told her, smiling at the memory. "All of us."

Her eyes lit up. "Really?"

He nodded. "Mmhmm. Every one of us knew that he'd only made it worse. Skeet knew it too. And your dad just laughed at all of us."

Rachel was quiet for a moment but was still smiling. "He did?"

David nodded again. "Yep. Papa Charlie just sat us all down and made us his famous grilled-cheese sandwiches. He said something like, 'Never get between a woman and the thing she wants most, boys. You'll only make her want it more.'"

"And he was right," Rachel said, her smile a mixture of nostalgia and amusement. "That's exactly what happened."

"Then may I never get in your way," David replied with a wink.

Rachel leaned a little closer, skyrocketing his pulse. "I don't believe you will."

He could have kissed her right then and there, and he desperately wanted to. He could almost . . .

"Strawberry, banana, *and* Nutella pancakes, side of hash browns." Paul set Rachel's plate down in front of her, and she sat back.

Wow, this place was warmer than he remembered.

He wiped at his brow as subtly as he could while Paul put his order in front of him and the biscuits and gravy between them, acting as another barrier.

"Ah, yes," Rachel sighed as she eyed the food. "This is perfect."

David looked up at her and caught the flick of her eyes to him.

Yes, it was perfect. It really was.

"You want to come to my game this afternoon?" he heard himself ask.

Rachel grinned very slowly. "I'd love to."

CHAPTER 5

"WOULD YOU LOOK at these seats? It's like being on the field itself! Oh my word, I can see right into the dugout. Please tell me you can get me Chad Lima's number."

Rachel fussed with the bill of her newly purchased Pittsburgh Knights cap and rolled her eyes just a little. "Megs . . ."

Meghan looked back at her, eyes wide with excitement, her perfect eyeliner fixed in place. "What? You're dating the primo hottie on the team, and I intend to take full advantage of that. Chad Lima is man meat, and I am one heck of a carnivore."

Well, that was blunt enough.

Rachel laughed and sat in her almost but not quite comfortable seat, sliding her crossbody bag off and tucking it beneath her. "I am not dating Grizz. We went to breakfast this morning, and that's it."

"And he saved you from your date, consequently turning it into another one," Meghan pointed out. "And you've been grinning ever since you got back from Eddie's."

"There's good food there. Good food makes me happy."

Meghan scoffed loudly, removed her own hat, and teased her hair. "Girl, you go ahead and live in denial. Twenty bucks says when Hottie McCarthy takes the field, he looks right up here at you."

"You're on," Rachel shot back, crossing her legs and grinning wide.

Her friend replaced her hat and tied her oversized jersey into a crop top.

"Oh come on," Rachel protested. "Why? Seriously, why?"

"Chad. Lima." Meghan looked up at her briefly as she continued to tie it. "Dead serious, girl. Help a sister out, huh? You watch the catcher; I'm gonna drool over first base."

"Knock yourself out." Rachel scanned the field as the Knights warmed up, smiling at the various antics of certain players whose names she'd heard here and there since she'd lived in Pittsburgh. It was strange; she had grown up watching baseball more often than she cared to admit and had gone to some of her brother's games after college, but she could honestly say that she couldn't remember when the last one was.

It would have been only too easy for her to hate baseball after so many years of forced game watching.

But she didn't.

She loved baseball.

Rachel pulled out her phone and snapped a selfie, then sent it to the Six Pack. Somehow, she still had all of their numbers, and though she didn't communicate with them often, lately she had been. Ever since her mom's wedding, when she had reconnected with them, she'd sent the occasional message, usually after seeing a great highlight.

Or a terrible one.

She didn't have to wait long for responses.

Sawyer: WHAT ARE YOU WEARING?

Levi: Take that awful hat off now!

Cole: Naw, baby girl, you've got the wrong team!

Ryker: You look beautiful, Sis.

Axel: Rabbit, stop sucking up. That hat's a crime against baseball.

Sawyer: You have Black Racer hats, I know you do. Where's your loyalty?

"Girl, how many guys are you stringing along?" Meghan demanded, finally taking her seat beside Rachel. "You haven't had a boyfriend since Troy, the Loser of All the Earth, and now your phone is blowing up while we're waiting to watch the Glory of All Catchers. Whatever you're taking, I need it too."

Rachel laughed and waved her phone at Meghan. "It's just the Six Pack, Megs. No boyfriends."

"'Just the Six Pack,' she says," Meghan muttered, shaking her head and waving down a guy selling popcorn. "Good night, woman. What it must be like to live your life."

"Oh, so glamorous," Rachel replied in a similar tone, watching as the Knights jogged back to the dugout. She looked down at her phone and typed out a quick response.

If Cole lets me borrow the jet, I'll come to your games too. But only my favorites.

That got them talking again, and she dropped her phone into her bag with a fond smirk.

Boys will be boys.

"Hey, I don't know you ladies."

Rachel looked up at a perfect Barbie doll of a woman with a face full of makeup, smiling with unnaturally flawless and blindingly white teeth.

"No, this is our first time," Rachel answered as she stood up. "I'm Rachel."

The woman held out her hand to shake, but kept it limp

as Rachel attempted to shake it. "Tawny Barnes. My husband is Troy Barnes, one of the relievers. I'm the unofficial wives liaison."

"We're not wives," Rachel said with a fixed smile. "Not even girlfriends."

Tawny's perfect brow furrowed in spite of any potential Botox injections to the area. "Then why are you sitting here? I don't mean to cause offense . . ."

"Sure you don't," Meghan grumbled so only Rachel could hear.

"But this section is traditionally for families and friends only." Tawny smiled again, though it was forced. "So who do you know?"

"Make her a list, Rach," came Meghan's snarky commentary.

Rachel's fixed smile was beginning to hurt. "I'm friends with Grizz."

Tawny's jaw dropped, and the line of her perky pink lipstick's edge seemed somehow amusing. "Grizz? He's never had anyone come to a game for him, not a single one. I didn't think he had people . . . Well, you know what I mean. He's just a loner."

"His parents like the third-base line," Rachel told her in a tight and would-be polite tone "And they're great."

Tawny shrugged as if she wasn't convinced. "I've never met them, and I'm at every game. Maybe they're not a close family."

A snarl rose within Rachel so fast she ought to have been on Animal Planet somewhere. "Third-base line," she ground out again, emphasizing each word. "That's where they sit whenever they come, and they come *often*. His younger brother is in the Marines and has been deployed for almost a year. His older brothers still live in Chicago and have five kids between them, so getting out to Pittsburgh is a bit tough, but they never miss a game when he plays near them. There's also some cousins in Chicago, and one whom I believe is in Columbus, and the only reason I know that is because when Grizz plays my brother, Sawyer Bennett, in Columbus, Kyle goes to the game and joins them for drinks after. Personally, I've known Grizz since I was fifteen, I know how he likes his burgers, what his favorite donut is, the exact make and model of the truck he drives, and how long it takes him to go from clean-shaven to token beard, so yes, he gave me tickets to sit in the family and friends section because I qualify." She inhaled, exhaled, then let her smile relax. "Grizz has people. And I'm one of them. Any more questions?"

Tawny stared at her, wide-eyed, her mascara-coated lashes sticking together in clumps. "Enjoy the game, Miss Bennett. And tell your brother my husband is a big fan."

"Will do," Rachel replied without hesitation. "Thanks, Tawny."

When the woman left, Rachel sank back down into her seat and covered her face.

"You are a goddess among women, you know that?" Meghan rubbed soothing circles on her back.

"Really?" Rachel laughed dubiously and looked at her friend. "Giving a complete stranger a shutdown because she's Judging Barbie?"

Meghan patted her back once. "And called yourself one of Grizz's people. Does he know you're a people?"

"I don't know," Rachel murmured as she looked over at the dugout. "But I want to be."

Her shoulders were suddenly turned, and Meghan stared at her, gripping her tightly. "Rachel Grace Bennett, did you just say you want to be on the list of Grizz McCarthy's people?"

It sounded totally crazy and completely irrational, and it went against anything she vowed, officially or not. Grizz was supposed to be off limits.

And yet . . .

"Maybe," Rachel admitted, screwing up her face.

Meghan began to laugh, but the sound was lost as the announcer broke the general noise of the fans to announce the starting lineups, and the national anthem started. Everyone rose and let the music play out, applauding at the end as usual.

"Ladies and gentlemen, now taking the field, your Pittsburgh Knights!"

The applause increased dramatically, though the stands were only maybe half full. It was a rough year for the Knights, and from Rachel's experience, there were a lot of fair-weather fans for this team. Rachel and Meghan cheered with the crowd as the players headed onto the field.

Rachel watched as Grizz and his starting pitcher jogged over from the bullpen, and she found herself smiling involuntarily at him. He wasn't even looking in her direction, laughing with his pitcher, and she still . . .

Grizz looked up into the stands then, rampant smile on his face, shining through his moderately short beard.

And he looked right at Rachel.

No searching, no hesitation.

Right at her.

Well. She owed Meghan twenty bucks.

She would be happy to turn it over.

She might have imagined it, but she swore that his grin grew, and she pointedly clapped for him, grinning right back.

Grizz winked, of all things, and saluted her, then continued to jog to home plate. He chatted with the umpire for a moment, then jumped a few times, hiking his knees to his chest exactly three times.

Rachel giggled at seeing it.

"What?" Meghan asked at once. "Watching Sexy Grizz jump is funny?"

"No, it's just . . ." Rachel shook her head. "He's always done that. That's his thing, but only at the beginning of the game. He's already warmed up, but he just does that. Told me once it was for good luck."

"Honey, that man doesn't need any more good luck than what God has already given him. Mmm." Meghan grunted in appreciation, and tossed popcorn into her mouth. "Lucky, lucky man. Ooh, look, there's my next boyfriend. Go, Chad! I love you, baby!"

Rachel nudged her friend hard. "Stop that, he could be married."

"He's not," Meghan assured her. "I checked."

Grizz called something to his pitcher, but his words were unintelligible as he pointed his glove at the guy. He glanced over his shoulder, back at her, still smiling, then pulled his mask down and squatted into his position.

Rachel felt her cheeks flame and exhaled very, very slowly.

Meghan nudged her popcorn box at Rachel. "Buck up, kiddo. You get to stare at some rather delicious buns for nine straight innings."

"Stop that!" Rachel scolded. "Come on, it's not like that."

"Uh, it's *exactly* like that." She turned to Rachel and propped her sunglasses up on her hat. "How'd you know all that info about Grizz's family? That was a lot."

Rachel shrugged uneasily, rubbing one arm, though she wasn't cold. "I've known Grizz for years. I guess I just remembered stuff, but . . . I don't know, that Tawny woman made it sound like he was some sort of hermit or loser, and he's not. He's anything but that, and he's from a great family.

He's the nicest guy in the world, and he makes me laugh, makes everyone laugh. He's the . . . the coach on the field, sort of. Sawyer always told me that Grizz is the cool head, the one who sets the vibe and centers the team. He's the one they turn to."

For some completely inexplicable reason, Rachel found herself getting almost emotional. She had to swallow a few times and blink twice as much.

She didn't realize she had strong feelings about Grizz besides the recent physical attraction. She'd always liked him, respected him, enjoyed being with him, but this . . .

Her emotions where he was concerned were confusing at the present, but they were deep and intense.

She watched him play for a few moments in silence, smiling whenever he did something great, which tended to be a lot. He really was a fantastic player, and he deserved to play for someone better than the Knights. They weren't a horrible team, but they certainly had none of the magic of last season.

That must have been hard for David, knowing where they had been and seeing where they were now. Losing some of their best players and being one of the few that remained. He hadn't said anything about it at breakfast or either of the other times they'd seen each other lately.

They hadn't talked about anything in particular.

They had just . . . talked.

And she'd loved it.

Funny thing was that Rachel wasn't that much of a talker, and David wasn't either. They weren't shy at all, but they weren't social butterflies.

But together they could talk. They could just be Rachel and David, not Sis and Grizz.

Just them.

And she loved being them.

But . . . when had he become more David and less Grizz?

He was Grizz, of course, but this was more. *He* was more.

"You're going to need to breathe one of these days, sweetie."

Rachel shook herself and looked at Meghan in embarrassment. "Sorry, lost in my thoughts."

"With that guy on the brain? Yeah, I would be too." Meghan grinned and raised her brows suggestively. "Tell me something. What did he wear to breakfast this morning?"

"A Henley," Rachel told her with a smile. "Oatmeal colored. Dark jeans, leather jacket."

Meghan fanned herself and pretended to dab at perspiration. "Lawd, have mercy," she drawled in a faux Southern accent.

"Basically." Rachel smirked at the memory. "It was a fantastic breakfast, Megs. So comfortable, and yet so uncomfortable. I don't know, it's not even real. Nothing's even happening officially, and yet . . ."

"Oh, things are happenin', all right, hey!" Meghan put her hands in the air and pumped them to the music blaring as the inning came to an end. "Things are happenin', Miss Bennett, and Mr. McCarthy is making them happen!"

Rachel covered her friend's mouth with a laugh. "Knock it off! People are going to hear you!"

Meghan jerked out of her grasp and swatted at her. "After your little stunt with Mrs. Relief Pitcher over there, the whole Wives Club will be talking about how you staked your claim. You and Grizz are a thing, babe, officially designated or not."

They weren't a thing, they couldn't be a thing.

Could they?

Rachel's hands flew to her cheeks and slowly fell to her lap. "Meghan . . . What am I going to tell my brother?"

"Psht." Meghan rolled her eyes, and Rachel could

actually hear them do so. "You tell Skeeter that no woman in her right mind is going to pass up a man like that when he shows an interest, and that you are a strong, gorgeous, freaking fantastic catch of a woman who don't need no big brother to tell her not to date his bestie."

"We're not dating," Rachel insisted without thinking.

Meghan shoved a handful of popcorn into her mouth, nodding as she chewed. "Uh-huh. Good. Go with that line, it works every time." She sat up with interest. "Ooh, hello, Rebels third baseman. Mama likes those thighs. Mmm. Remind me to move to DC."

"Right, right." Rachel waved that off as she eyed the dugout as surreptitiously as possible. She couldn't remember where he fell in the batting lineup, if the lineup remained the same, or anything.

David suddenly appeared, hanging over the dugout fence loosely with some teammates. He glanced over at her again, and, again, he smiled.

Again, she smiled back.

"You're in trouble, Rach," Meghan said without much emotion. "You're in deep, deep trouble."

"I know," Rachel murmured, continuing to smile at David. "I know."

Chapter 6

Belltown was a special place, something unlike any place David had ever lived. It held the energy of every sporting event ever hosted in its air, and its traditions lived and breathed among the students that walked its campus.

He inhaled deeply and sighed a satisfied exhale. "I love this place."

"No kidding," Rabbit replied as he walked beside him towards the field. "You're practically crying with every step."

"Am not." David nudged him hard, laughing. "Come on, man, you're telling me your heart isn't just a little bit lighter taking this path again?"

Rabbit said nothing for a moment, strolling along in his skinny jeans and Sperrys, perfect hair and perfect color coordination. If there was one thing that anyone could say about Ryker Stone, it was that the man knew how to dress, and he did it exceptionally well.

David wouldn't have been caught dead in some of the snazzy things Rabbit wore, but David preferred sweats to anything else in his wardrobe.

He was wearing sweats now, actually.

Belltown ones.

Heave-ho.

"Yeah, all right," Rabbit finally conceded. "I'm feeling like singing 'Hail to Belltown' right about now, and it would be a doozy."

David threw his arm around Rabbit's shoulders and patted his chest. "Atta boy, come on, let's sing it out!"

"No," Rabbit deadpanned.

"TIMBERLINE!" a familiar voice bellowed just ahead of them.

Rabbit snorted. "How did that lunatic get here before we did?"

"I've given up trying to understand anything where Big Dawg is concerned," David told him with a shrug. "But hey, the others will be here as soon as they pick up the food. Ten bucks Skeeter forgets my onion rings."

"I don't take bets I know I'm gonna lose." Rabbit turned down the stairs and fake punched Big Dawg in the stomach as he stood holding the door to the baseball clubhouse at Ackerman Field.

David *did* punch Dawg in the stomach, though not hard.

"Hey now," Dawg protested with a fake wince. "Don't hate because I'm number five and you're number eight."

"If your abs were as good as mine," David informed him calmly as he walked past, "that wouldn't have hurt."

"Oh, now that is just wrong." Dawg closed the door and followed as the three of them headed up to the clubhouse.

"Doesn't mean it's not true," Rabbit called over his shoulder. "Your core has always been your weakness, Dawg."

David was rather fond of Rabbit. He really ought to tell his new favorite member of the Six Pack that. He deserved to know such a compliment.

"Bite your tongue, Cottontail," Dawg snarled as they entered the clubhouse, flopping himself down on one of the couches.

David looked around the room, smiling at how unchanged it was from when they had been here. There had been some updates to the photos on the wall, but the traditional ones remained. Ben Ackerman's poster hung where it always had, the photo of the championship team from 1992 hung over one couch, and the historic black-and-white photo of a full team of actual lumberjacks from Belltown spanned the entire western wall.

The TVs were updated, as was all of the equipment in the room, but the couches were the same. The fridge full of sports drinks was the same. The cupboards full of snacks were the same.

One noted difference was that now there was a framed poster of the Six Pack next to Ben Ackerman's.

The man the baseball park at Belltown was named after. Baseball Hall of Famer and the face of the Atlanta Falcons franchise.

The guy was a legend.

And they were up there with him.

David shook his head and moved to sit on the couch by Rabbit. "How did we manage access to the clubhouse, any-way?"

Rabbit waved a hand. "Skeeter said please, and Dawg made a donation. Besides, they love us. We could probably play on the field if we wanted to."

"Doubt Coach Maxwell would like that," Dawg broke in with a chuckle. "Not even on his Hall of Fame weekend. No extra time on the field, remember?"

David laughed at the same time his phone buzzed, and he checked the screen.

Rachel: Hey, hope you're having a blast. Can't wait to see you tomorrow. Save me the seat next to you at dinner.

A sharp burst of heat exploded somewhere in the vicinity

of his heart, and he stared at the text for longer than was appropriate or necessary. He'd seen her just yesterday, when they had washed their cars together at a place down the street from his condo, and never had washing cars been so entertaining.

Or so attractive.

What had possessed him to consider that a viable way to spend an afternoon with Rachel? They'd been doing this tentative dance around each other for a full week and change, always managing to avoid anything actually resembling a traditional date. But a car wash?

It had worked out well, considering Rachel had sprayed him with water within the first ten minutes. Being the competitive sort, he had returned the favor, and the most epic water fight of his life had commenced. Soap and bubbles got into the mix, and upon reflection, he was pretty sure that his truck and her car didn't actually get all that clean.

He could still see Rachel laughing her head off, slumping against his truck, her hair drenched and dripping. David had leaned beside her, his Knights T-shirt clinging to his skin, bubbles tangled in his beard. He'd pushed his classic aviators on top of his head, not wanting anything shielding Rachel from his sight in all her glory.

They'd almost kissed then. And by almost he meant they had stared at each other's lips for more than four heartbeats.

His heart skipped just at the memory.

Then, when they'd left and he'd given her a hug, she'd turned her head to say something, he'd turned his head to listen, neither of them had moved far enough away, and . . .

He could still feel that almost brush of their lips, and his mind went blank, just as it had then.

Awkward aversion of eyes, hesitant stepping back, she'd tucked some hair behind her ear, and then . . .

She'd looked right at him, smiled, and giggled. "Well, David . . . Remind me to wash my car more often."

He couldn't remember what he'd said, but he felt exactly the same way.

Exactly.

He texted Rachel back quickly.

Having fun, but it will be better when you're here. The seat next to me is yours.

He pocketed his phone and sat there for a second, grinding his teeth just a little in thought.

He wasn't sure how much longer he could avoid the obvious, but there was one thing he had to know before he did anything.

"Question, boys," David said suddenly, keeping his voice as calm as he could. "On a scale of spit in my food to burying pieces of my body in the backyard, how upset would Skeeter be about . . . my going on a date with Rachel?"

Dawg and Rabbit both jerked their heads to stare at him with wide eyes. "With . . . Sis?" Big Dawg asked with some trepidation.

David nodded, swallowing. "Yeah."

"Bro code," Rabbit told him with a shake of his head. "Sis should be off limits."

"Right." David swallowed again. "Right, I know that. But . . ."

"Are we talking *a* date?" Dawg demanded, overriding him. "Singular? Or a series of dates, plural? Or are we talking something in the 'other' category?"

David clamped down on his lips, sat forward, and rubbed his hands together. "Honestly, we're probably talking *other* category. It . . . could be serious."

Dawg and Rabbit gave each other horrified looks, then returned their attention to him. "Would you like Skeet to punch you with your aviators on or off?" Dawg inquired with mild interest. "Would you like to be buried in Belltown or back home in Joliet? And, out of curiosity, have you kissed her yet?"

"Dawg, we are not encouraging this," Rabbit told him, chucking a random baseball in his direction that Dawg caught easily.

"Why not?" came the heavily twanged reply. Dawg leveled David with a serious look. "May I say, in case I forget, and without anyone else overhearing . . . Nicely done, my man. And if you tell anyone I said that, I will sue you for defamation."

David gaped at his friend. "Wait, what?"

"You think that no one in the Six Pack noticed how grown up Rachel looked at Mamma Sal's wedding? Believe me, we all noticed." Big Dawg smiled very slightly. "Not that we're dumb enough to do anything about it."

Rabbit continued to shake his head, sitting up. "Noticing that Sis is an adult and a stunning woman and actually wanting to have a romantic relationship with her are two very different things." He looked at David with a mixture of disgust and warning. "I'd gut you if you came anywhere near Bree."

"You would not," Dawg groaned as he got up to open the door to the clubhouse, the sound of footsteps echoing. "Grizz is a good guy with a steady job, a college education, and no criminal record that anybody knows of. Your mom would love to have him for Bree."

"This is not for public consumption," David insisted as the door opened.

"Right," Dawg agreed with a nod. He stepped back to let Axe Man in. "Just you?"

Axe Man handed him a large paper bag. "He's not far behind me. Skeet forgot the onion rings, so he went back to get them."

David gestured dramatically to Rabbit, who only rolled his eyes. "Figures."

"What isn't for public consumption?" Axe asked as he carried another bag over to the table.

Rabbit grinned like a cat with cream. "Grizz wants Sis."

Axe whirled to face David with round eyes. "Whoa!"

"Come on, Rabbit," David groaned, putting his head in his hands. "I said not to . . ."

"What's the fuss?" Steal asked as he strode in.

Dawg waved at David. "Grizz has the hots for Sis."

Steal looked over at him in surprise but nodded. "Right on."

"Say what?" one of them said as David eyed Steal with some suspicion.

Of all the guys, he was not the one that he'd thought would go for this.

Axe started laughing and folded his arms as he leaned against the table. "Now who has the great pleasure of informing Skeet that Grizz and Sis are an item?"

"Hold on, hold on," David protested, holding his hands up to stop the nonsense. "We are not!"

"Details," Axe scoffed with a shrug. "You will be. And Skeet's gonna have some interesting thoughts on the subject."

That's what he was afraid of.

David winced. "Think so?"

"Grizz." Steal came over and put a hand on his shoulder. "There is only one thing that Skeeter cares about more than his Mustang. That would be his family."

"Boys," Rabbit said, rising from the couch, "please remove your hats while we have a moment of silence in anticipation of the death of our brother, Grizz, formerly known as David McCarthy."

David shook his head, staring around at the lot of them.

"You all are really being so helpful. So supportive. Couldn't do it without you."

Axe clicked his tongue then. "Well, if you couldn't do it without us, then you really shouldn't even try for Sis, man. That's just pathetic."

"So you're saying that I should try?"

"I'm saying that you need to be prepared to grovel," Axe told him, sounding serious even though he was smiling broadly. "Full on kneeling, possibly crawling-over-glass groveling."

David nodded very slowly, confusion and tension coursing through him. "Right, right. What would you do?"

"If it were Silvia?" Axel shrugged one shoulder. "Tell me before it gets too far. Maybe ask if that's okay. But if my sister wants to and I know you're a good guy, I've got no reason to say no."

A ray of hope entered David's mind, and he stared at his friend with that same hope. "Really?"

Axel nodded. "Sure. But if you did hurt her, I would end you in ways you couldn't possibly comprehend. So if it's worth the risk, go for it."

That was just it. That was the problem.

It *was* worth the risk.

Rachel was worth everything.

But what would it cost him?

"Nobody tell Skeet," David warned the group. "This is my thing, you hear me?"

They all nodded, smiles of varying degrees on each of their faces.

He wouldn't put it past one of them, or a couple of them, dropping major hints to Skeeter about David's intentions, but they wouldn't come right out and say anything.

Small mercies.

The door to the clubhouse opened again, and this time it was Skeeter who walked through the door. "Sorry, sorry, I brought the onion rings," he said, waving the bag at them all. "Now let's down all of this before any of the young'uns decide to use their clubhouse."

Hours later, David sat alone in the darkened kitchen of Mamma Sal's house, unable to sleep and mulling over far too many things. He shouldn't have agreed to stay here, though there was no arguing with Mamma Sal about anything. And he had no reason to refuse, considering there wasn't anything to tell.

But Rach would be in tomorrow, and she would be staying here. They wouldn't spend even one night under the same roof, as David and Big Dawg had to take the jet that night to LA for the series between the Knights and the Sea Rays, but for some reason, it still felt dangerous.

What if he couldn't control the way he looked at Rachel? The way he talked to her, how often he smiled when she was around, or how he noticed practically everything she did? It was like he needed to be brought up on stalking charges, aside from the actual lack of stalking.

Mentally stalking? Was that a thing? He wasn't tempted to go stand outside of her place and wait for her to come out, but he always wanted to be near her, to be where she was.

He'd been in plenty of relationships in his life, though none recently, and he'd never felt this level of desperation about it.

And desperate was exactly how he felt. He leaned his elbows on the table and rubbed his face.

This was insanity, the whole thing.

And it was incredibly distracting.

"Couldn't sleep?"

David looked up to see Mamma Sal leaning against the

fridge, wearing a sweatshirt and flannel pants, smiling gently at him.

He returned the smile. "Apparently not. You?"

"Oh, at my age I only sleep in three-hour bursts," she assured him with her usual motherly smile. "But a cup of cocoa and some toast with peanut butter always sets me to rights. Would you like some?"

David chuckled and ran a hand through his hair. "Actually, that sounds great, Mamma."

She smiled further and walked by him to the stove, patting him on the back as she did so. "You got it."

"Todd still sleeping?" David asked, turning in the chair to face her.

Mamma Sal laughed and gave him a dry look. "The man could sleep through a war. I've never seen anything like it. All of my tossing and turning never even makes him flinch."

She said all of this with a smile, and there was a tenderness in her look that made David smile back at her.

"You seem really happy, Mamma Sal," he murmured. "It's great."

His words seemed to surprise her for a second, then she swallowed hard. "Thank you, David. I am happy. I didn't know if I could be after Charlie died, but Todd . . ." She sighed and leaned against the counter. "Todd patches the holes and fixes the cracks. And I hope I do the same for him."

David gave a soft laugh. "I'm sure you do. You're Mamma Sal. Everybody knows you're the best."

That earned him a wry look. "Your mother is way more impressive than I am, David. Aubrey McCarthy is one of a kind."

He shrugged. "You are both card-carrying members of the same club. Not a contest."

Mamma Sal clicked her tongue. "For that, you get some

of my hidden stash of banana bread." She moved to the cupboard and moved aside a box of cereal, then pulled down a carefully wrapped partial loaf of banana bread, waving it at him.

David heaved a delighted sigh. "I love you, Mamma Sal."

She chuckled and moved back to the stove, pulling the kettle off. "I love you, too, sweetheart. Don't you dare tell Sawyer I have this."

"I promise," David vowed, crossing his heart.

Mamma Sal cut him a slice and brought it over to him on a plate, then made the cocoa and set down a Belltown mug before him, the steam of the cocoa rising slowly above it.

David grunted softly, eying the mug. "Nice touch." He raised his mug and touched it to hers, then suddenly realized that Mamma Sal was Rachel's mother, and just as suddenly, he was on edge.

Not that he would ever be anything less than comfortable in her presence, but knowing how he felt about Rachel made every thought he had and word he said more important.

More telling.

More private.

What would Mamma Sal think?

This woman was his second mother, and there wasn't much he had ever hidden from her in all the time he had known her.

Of course, it helped that Mamma Sal was one of the most intuitive people on the planet, but still.

"David," the woman in question said quietly, breaking into his thoughts with perfect timing. "I can hear you overthinking from here."

"I never overthink," he replied with a forced smile, scratching at the tattoo on his right arm, which was a sure sign of his nerves. "I always think just the right amount."

She laughed once. "Tell that to a woman who doesn't have a head case for a son and a champion overthinker for a daughter."

"No," he drawled slowly, widening his eyes for effect. He snickered then and sipped his cocoa. "Just a lot on my mind. I'm fine."

Mamma Sal nodded slowly before looking down into her cocoa thoughtfully. "My daughter talks to me often, David. I know you two have been seeing each other."

David nearly choked on his cocoa. "We're . . . we're not dating."

Mamma Sal's blue eyes flicked to his as her lips quirked into a smile. "I didn't say you were."

Dang. She hadn't, had she?

Classic overplaying.

Idiot.

He winced and looked away. "Does Skeeter know?"

"No. And I don't plan on telling him."

David glanced over at her in hesitation. "No?"

Mamma Sal shook her head. "You and Rachel are adults, and I'm not standing on the porch with a shotgun waiting for you. I love you, David. You're like a son to me. And if you can make Rachel happy, and she can do the same for you, nothing would make *me* happier."

Was that . . . was she giving him the go-ahead? With Rachel?

He exhaled very slowly. "I don't know where it will go. I don't even know *if* it will go. I just . . . I want to try. I really . . . really want to try."

"Hmm," Mamma Sal mused, laughing to herself. "I think you will find, sweetheart, that Rachel wants to try as well."

David stared at Mamma Sal for a long minute, his heart pounding somewhere in the middle of his back. "Really?" he asked, unable to stop smiling.

Mamma Sal sipped her cocoa, now smiling back at him. "Really, David. Take her to the banquet tomorrow. I'll take care of Sawyer."

Sensing he had the best ally he could possibly wish for, David nodded once, then held his mug out again to clink against hers.

CHAPTER 7

"LADIES AND GENTLEMEN, welcome to the forty-third annual Belltown University Hall of Fame banquet!"

Polite applause filled the room, and Rachel smiled at Mr. Walters, the athletic director, standing on the dais they'd set up in the athletic banquet hall. He was dressed in a tuxedo, as were all of the men in the room, and his ready smile was easy to return.

"I won't waste too much of your time, since I know the catering staff has something special planned for us," he went on, smiling over at the kitchens. "Tonight we honor former women's volleyball middle blocker Teresa Jenkins Jersey; former linebacker Mark Preston; former men's diver Cary Markham; former gymnast Sandi Benson Alton; and legendary current baseball coach, Rich Maxwell."

Applause filled the room again, along with a few whistles as the inductees stood at their table near the front of the room, waving to the other guests.

The athletic director clapped, then leaned into the microphone. "We'll get to the actual honors and speeches in a bit. For now, eat up and enjoy the evening!"

Rachel smiled and turned back to the table, her leg brushing against David's as she did so.

They both stilled, and she reached for her ice water, her second glass, wishing she had even colder ice cream.

Neither of them had said much tonight, and the butterflies in her stomach were unbearable. David looked impossibly good in his tux, perfectly tailored and pristine. Her throat had gone just as dry at the sight of him as it had when she'd seen his picture in *Sports Monthly*.

This was why she had spent way more money than she should have on the dress she was wearing, a long, form-fitting gown with a deep scoop in the back and a higher scoop to the neckline.

She had to match David. She had to *impress* David.

Hopefully she'd done that.

Her mother had managed to get Sawyer out of the way before the banquet, asking him to take her and Todd over to the florist to pick up something she'd ordered for Coach Maxwell, which had left David and Rachel alone in the house. Rachel had kept to her room and prepped. And paced.

When he'd finally called up to her, asking if she was ready, she'd tentatively made her way down. She'd never worked this hard on her hair or her makeup, and she had been positive her lungs had never felt quite that tight.

David had openly gaped when he saw her, which had made her cheeks flame, but she had smiled all the same. "You remembered," he'd breathed.

"Remembered?" she had asked him.

His slow nod had heated her from the inside out. "That I love the way you look in red."

Her cheeks began to heat even now as she remembered, sitting beside him. How would she possibly manage to get through this night and still have any sanity left?

"Hey, Sis," Ryker said from across the table, smiling at her the way he usually did. "How's Pittsburgh?"

She smiled back at him. "It's growing on me."

David shifted next to her, and she felt him drawing closer, his hand immediately dropping between them and brushing along her chair. Slowly, desperate to avoid the obvious, she moved her hand in that direction, weaving her fingers between his.

The touch of skin on skin sent fire racing up her arm, and for a moment, she felt almost light-headed.

David rubbed his thumb against hers, and a slow exhale of calm escaped her.

"How's the dance company?" Ryker went on, taking a bite of his steak. "You liking it?"

Rachel shrugged once. "It's a nice group, and the programs are really beautiful. It's not quite what I wanted, but New York didn't quite pan out, so I'm just happy to dance."

"That makes me sad," Cole drawled, buttering a roll. "You deserve the big time, Sis."

"You're sweet," she replied. "But it didn't happen. I'm considering teaching dance instead of dancing myself. Might get me out of working the side job, if I do it right."

She could feel David's attention on her, but she couldn't look at him. "Are you going to eat?" he whispered.

"Are you going to let go of my hand?" she countered in the same tone.

He squeezed her hand almost painfully tight, then slowly released it, and, very carefully, she began to eat.

"You'd be a fantastic teacher, Rach," Sawyer commented from the other side of Todd and their mom, sitting between them.

Rachel quirked her brows in amusement. "You never know. Anyway." She smiled over at Levi, trying for mischief. "How's Minnesota, Levi?"

He groaned while the table laughed, and conversation steered away from her for a while, which was perfect. All she wanted to do was relax and enjoy being dressed up, sitting next to David, and hold his hand again.

Managing to actually eat the catered dinner before her seemed almost inconsequential by comparison.

Rationally speaking, she knew they couldn't hold hands the entire night, but she could pretend it was possible.

"Grizz, are the Knights going to do something this season?" Axel asked with a teasing grin. "Or are you guys just gonna stick to being underdogs?"

"Ooh, not nice, Axe," Levi hissed as he sawed into his asparagus. "Grizz is doing the best he can, but until he gets that call to the Spades or the Flames, he'll go wherever the game is."

"Like Minnesota?" Sawyer laughed, giving his friend a pointed look.

Levi returned it with a glower. "Exactly."

Rachel looked at David then, her brow creasing. "Chicago teams?"

He shrugged, looking a little sheepish. "It's always been my dream to play for one of the Chicago teams. Hometown thing, you know? Plus they're always contenders in their divisions." He tossed a grin at Sawyer. "Maybe it's my turn to be the hometown hero."

The Six Pack chortled their opinions on that, but Rachel couldn't stop staring at David. Of course he would want to play for a Chicago team; why wouldn't he? Chicago was his home, and he would have grown up watching them. It would have been amazing for him to play for them, but what were the odds?

"Is it possible to get on with one of them?" she quietly asked him, her voice almost a whimper as her hand dropped between them again. He took it at once.

She couldn't lose him. She didn't even have him, but she couldn't lose him.

He met her eyes, their impossible blueness all the brighter against the dark of his tuxedo. "Always possible. I still have two years on my contract with Pittsburgh, but they need to build, so they might talk with some other teams. As far as I know, no one has asked yet. Honestly, I . . . I would love to get out of Pittsburgh. Anywhere would do. That's what I was meeting with my agent about the other night."

His meeting with Marcus. He was talking about leaving Pittsburgh.

He wanted to leave.

Rachel stared at him, knowing her heart was in her eyes. He stared at her with the same intensity. Suddenly their hold on each other's hands became clenching.

Maybe he didn't want to leave.

The thought crashed into her mind with terrifying poignancy. He clearly wanted to play for a better team, even if he was happy to be playing at all. And there were options for him. If things worked out, he could play for any team out there.

Their situations weren't so different, then.

Only she couldn't dance for any company out there.

She was stuck where she was.

But this hold he had on her, and not just on her hand, gave her hope.

For what, she didn't know.

But he was holding her hand almost painfully tight.

And that was a glorious thing.

Conversation swirled around them, and they managed to participate, but the small distance between them seemed suddenly charged, even when their hands were not touching. They laughed and joked with the others, but Rachel, for one, was forcing most of it.

She had to.

The program started shortly after, and the inductees were introduced by former teammates or coaches, making jokes and telling stories that made the entire room laugh. Rachel had been tempted more than once to lean against David's shoulder, and she knew he would have let her, or even put his arm around her.

That thought made it difficult to swallow, which, thankfully, David wouldn't be able to see.

Then, at last, it was Coach Maxwell's turn, and the Six Pack got up from the table and headed up to the dais, earning applause from the rest of the guests.

"Hello, Belltown!" Cole greeted, waving broadly. "Did you miss us?"

The room laughed, and Sawyer stepped forward. "Thanks for inviting us here tonight. I don't think Coach Maxwell is that excited, not after what we put him through. He may need another ten years before he cracks a smile when he sees us."

Laughter rang out, and Rachel chanced a look at the coach, who was, true to form, not smiling, though he was close to it.

"If there's one thing we learned from Coach over the years," Sawyer went on, clearly taking the lead in this, "it's that there is no such thing as an individual champion in baseball. Some may get awards, some may get more acknowledgement . . ."

Cole raised his hand, and David cuffed him on the back of the head, making the room roar with laughter.

Sawyer only shook his head. "But in the end, it is a team that wins. It is a team that loses. It is a team that fights to the end or gives up on the way. An individual's contribution to his team is important, but that is just one piece. One part. Over the years, Coach Maxwell has coached many individuals on many, many teams. He is a legend not only to Belltown, but to the sport of baseball as a whole. To talk more about that, and to tell even better stories than a night with the Six Pack could give you, we have the very great pleasure to present a surprise guest."

David suddenly stepped forward, grinning broadly. "Ladies and gentlemen, the hero of the entire Six Pack, and Belltown's real favorite baseball player, Mr. Ben Ackerman!"

The room was on its feet in a heartbeat, and the still handsome Ben Ackerman moved up to the dais, shook hands with every member of the Six Pack, pulling each in for a slap on the back, and waved at Coach Maxwell as the others returned to their seats. "Hi, Coach."

Coach Maxwell stunned the room by laughing, and he folded his arms, almost daring his former player to tell stories.

Rachel smiled at her brother as he walked by to return to his seat, and Sawyer winked, putting a hand on her shoulder and squeezing gently.

David was behind him, and he had his public smile fixed on his face now.

Then he looked at Rachel.

Her heart seemed to slow, and her body went numb. Pleasantly so, warmth cascading from the center of her chest out to her fingertips.

David's smile softened, and he rounded his chair on her side of it.

And his fingers brushed against her bare upper arm, sending a shiver through her that rippled across her entire body.

He thought that banquet would never end.

Oh, David had been thrilled to have the opportunity to

honor Coach Maxwell, and it was great to get together with the guys, as it always was. The food was the best catered meal he'd ever had, and some alumni at the event had said some very nice things to him.

But when he had seen Rachel come down the stairs at her house, the last thing he'd wanted to do was go to a banquet, surrounded by people, and pretend like he wasn't falling for her.

She was stunning. That was no surprise; she was always stunning, but tonight she had taken his breath away in a manner he had never felt before.

Her hesitant smile undid him. The red fabric flowing over her perfect curves distracted him. The scoop of her neckline called to him.

Then she had turned to grab a coat, revealing the back of the dress, and David had died on the spot.

Well, for the space of seven would-be heartbeats, anyway.

The dress scooped low, revealing shoulder blades, a toned back, and just a hint of the telltale dip just above her hips. The long chain of gold necklace hung directly down the middle of her back, drawing attention up the chain and down.

Impossibly beautiful. That's what Rachel Bennett was, and in that dress, she left no question.

Sitting next to her at dinner had been torment. Holding her hand had been exhilarating. The combination of the two had been a whirlwind.

He'd loved every minute of it.

Mamma Sal had intervened when the banquet had finally ended and asked him to take Rachel back to the house before heading to the airport with Cole. She'd immediately turned to Skeeter and asked if he minded running her to the grocery store before they headed back. Skeeter, being the obedient and indulgent son, had agreed.

David had hugged Mamma Sal especially tight before leaving.

Now he and Rachel were almost to the house, and they had barely said a word to each other.

David, for one, couldn't think of a single thing to say.

Several things ran through his mind as possibilities of what he *could* say, but nothing that he would actually risk saying out loud.

He could only exhale as silently as possible and hope that he didn't screw this up.

Whatever *this* was.

He pulled Todd's car up to the house, parking in front rather than in the driveway. He had to head to the airport to meet up with Big Dawg so they could get to LA late tonight, and he didn't have time to stick around. Todd would pick up his car tomorrow, he'd assured him, which saved David the trouble of renting.

He was rambling, even in his mind.

He put the car into park and sat there silently as he undid his bowtie.

Rachel didn't speak either.

"When are you back in Pittsburgh?" she eventually asked.

David cleared his throat. "Sunday, late. Then we're out again on Tuesday, then out for the weekend."

"Busy guy," she murmured. "Where are you going?"

"LA tonight. Then Atlanta on Tuesday, Michigan for the weekend." He leaned his head back against the headrest. "Then we're home for a stretch."

Rachel made a soft, noncommittal sound he couldn't read. "Well, have fun. I'll watch the games and cheer for you."

He rolled his head on the headrest to smile at her. "Thanks."

Her eyes met his. "I have a show next week. Want to come?"

"Of course. Send me the dates, and I'll see if something works."

Rachel only nodded. Then they stared at each other in silence.

"Well," she finally sighed, reaching for the door handle, "thanks for taking me home."

Now it was his turn to nod. "Of course. You looked . . . look . . . absolutely beautiful. In case I didn't mention that earlier."

A quick smile flashed across her full red lips. "Thanks. And by the way, I like you best in a tux." Before he could respond, she opened the door and stepped out of the car. "See you when you get back."

He opened his mouth to reply, but she pushed the door closed and began her walk up the drive to the dark house.

David watched her walk, marveling at how smoothly she managed to do so in the towering heels she had worn. He'd been told by his cousins that heels made a woman's legs seem longer and her silhouette sleeker. Rachel didn't need any help in either department, but he appreciated the effects all the same.

Rachel walked up the stairs to the porch, the light there giving her fair hair an almost heavenly look. She glanced over her shoulder at him as she unlocked the door, hesitated, then stepped into the house and closed the door behind her.

David stared at the closed front door, unable to look anywhere else. What was he doing? He'd thought of little else but kissing Rachel since she'd come down the stairs, and probably since they'd escaped her terrible date together. He had been given the perfect opportunity here, and he was just going to let her walk back into the house and go to bed? He was going to leave Belltown without anything happening between them?

Was he going to actively avoid any potential moments between them back in Pittsburgh too? Was he going to sit in a car and watch her move away from him, too much of a coward to do something about this feeling between them?

The porch light switched off then, and somehow, that did it.

"No," he grunted to himself, turning off the car, undoing his seatbelt, and throwing the car door open. Not checking to see if it had closed, he strode through the grass up to the house, taking the few stairs in half the number of steps.

The moment he reached the door, it was flung open, and Rachel stood there. She'd kicked off her heels, putting her a few inches shorter than she had been all evening.

At an even better height and angle for what he had planned.

She stepped out, her breathing unsteady, audible even to him.

David stared for a moment, his chest constricting and coiling into something hot. Her eyes were trained on his, unblinking, unwavering.

A faint exhale passed her parted lips.

He moved, and so did she. One of his hands slid into her hair while the other wrapped around her waist, both of her hands going to his face as their lips connected. Over and over, he kissed her, his mouth slanting against hers, around it, within it, and she matched him in every way. The world tilted on its axis, and David pressed Rachel backwards, moving her against the front of the house, anchoring them both while the tension within and between them rose and fell in almost painful surges.

Rachel pushed up to her toes, her arms wrapping around his neck tightly, deepening the kiss with reckless abandon. One of her hands slid down and fisted in the pristine linen of his shirt, and the muscles beneath constricted in response. His fingers moved against the silky smoothness of her dress, the feeling of her tight and toned back tensing beneath his touch sending jolts of electricity into his fingers.

Her teeth grazed against his bottom lip, and his hold on her tensed in response. He slid the hand in her hair to her jaw, his thumb stroking a steady pattern against her skin as he kissed her again and again, finding new aspects of her lips and mouth to explore and expose. She gasped against his lips, gripping his neck tightly as he slid his mouth along her jaw, back to the base of her ear.

The hand in his shirt slid around to his back, pressing against him with surprising force even as her other hand pulled him further in. His mouth raced back to hers for another, much slower onslaught. He groaned as her fingers slid to his beard, scraping gently against his jaw and chin.

He would never breathe, never think, never feel normal ever again. This was the end of life as he knew it, and the brilliance of the new dawn before him was blinding.

Once, twice, three or four times he kissed her again, slowly and tenderly attempting to bring this windswept sensation to heel, wanting to stay with all that he was, knowing he could not.

Rachel whimpered as their lips parted, touching her brow to his as ragged pants raged between them.

David exhaled, his body trembling against her without shame. "Rach . . ."

She sighed and nodded against him, her hand on his back sliding up and down in slow, even strokes. "Yeah. Just . . . yeah . . ."

"Uh-huh." He nuzzled against her, moving up to kiss her brow. "Damn . . ." he whispered against her skin.

Rachel giggled and pulled back, smiling dazedly up at

him. "Pretty much. Just before you marched up here, I was thinking that you should have kissed me. Or I should have kissed you. I watched from the window, thinking you were going to drive away."

His grin was slow. "I decided to take a chance. I knew what I wanted, I just wasn't sure what you wanted."

She scratched her fingers gently along his beard again, then tugged on one end of his loose bowtie. "Did I answer that well enough for you?"

David bent his head and kissed her very softly. "Yes." He brushed her lips one more time for good measure. "I have to go."

Rachel hummed and pushed up onto her tiptoes, pressing a tender kiss to his cheek. "Good night, David."

He held her to him, wrapping his arms around her slender body. "Good night, Rach."

She pressed her face into his shoulder for a moment. "Call me tomorrow?" she murmured.

He nodded against her. "Yeah. Every day until I'm back. I'm in this, babe."

She shivered and clung closer. "Me too."

He closed his eyes as a wave of bliss crashed over him, then, with more effort than it should have taken, he pried his arms from her and stepped back. "Bye."

Rachel smiled and waved a little. "Bye, handsome."

David laughed, backing down the steps. "You're going to watch me play, right?"

"Oh yeah," Rachel shot back. "I'm Team Grizz all the way."

He nodded, still grinning, and turned for the car, sliding in and turning it on in one almost-smooth motion. With a final wave to Rachel, he drove off, whistling like a lunatic as he headed for the airport.

It didn't take him long to get there and board the jet. Big Dawg was already there, jacket and bowtie gone, top buttons of his shirt undone, eyes closed. One of them cracked open as David sat in a chair across the aisle from him.

"So," he said without fanfare, "that took longer than it should have."

David shrugged out of his jacket. "Yep. I kissed Rachel."

Both of Dawg's eyes opened. "Did she kiss you back?"

"Yep," David responded, not bothering to hide his grin.

Big Dawg heaved a dramatic sigh. "Well, it was nice knowing you, Grizz."

Then he held out a fist across the aisle, not exactly fighting the smile that was spreading.

David laughed once, then bumped his fist to his friend's.

CHAPTER 8

"FIVE, SIX, SEVEN, and lift . . . *développé* and *soutinou*. *Cambré* forward, and turning *pas de bourrée*. Beautiful, beautiful. Keep going."

Rachel arched against Colby, letting him lift her right leg while hooking her left around his hips. He turned her around, then pushed up while she continued to arch, curling over his shoulder until her right leg pointed perfectly upward. Then, kicking her legs down, she tumbled gracefully down his back, landing on her knees, her hands finding his between his legs. Pulling, Colby tugged her through them and, once through, Rachel sprang to her feet before twirling and letting him cradle her in his arms.

"Nicely done, very nice." Monica clapped, her cat-eye glasses glinting in the lights of the stage. "Can we move ahead to the parallels?"

Colby straightened Rachel and exhaled, wiping his brow. "Guess so. I still can't match Rachel's height on the *saut de chat*. She's got a few inches on me."

Monica surprised them both by waving that off. "You've got three inches on her in height, so that should match you up with those. As long as it's tight and together, I don't care if she outjumps you."

"Nice!" Colby pumped his fist and grinned at Rachel before he moved to his mark.

Rachel tugged at her overshirt, which had begun to cling to the skin her leotard didn't cover. They'd been at this for three hours, and Monica had given every other number the all-clear to go. Show week wasn't supposed to be this intense, but Monica had never quite followed the pattern of the generally accepted way of things in the dance world. It was a risky way of running a company, but Andante was slowly building its reputation.

Still wasn't a big-time group, but the members in it were dedicated.

Rachel had to keep telling herself that.

"Parallels, here we go!" Doug, the assistant director, called from his corner, cheering in his most nasal of voices.

Rachel looked at Colby and the two of them mentally rolled their eyes.

No one cared for Doug. Except, it seemed, Monica.

Doug thought he was the artistic director of all Andante, despite only having responsibility for the things Monica gave him *when* she gave them to him. It didn't change his condescending manner or his intrusiveness, but it managed to keep him from completely taking over.

Shaking her head, Rachel moved to her mark and placed her left foot out perpendicular to her body, waiting.

"Five, six, seven, eight, *plié!*"

Rachel went into the pattern, spinning, flipping, and springing in the same formation she had been practicing for weeks now, and she could only hope that her partner in this number was doing the same. She could see him out of the corner of her eye, but she couldn't track him without losing her own motions.

"No, no, no, no!" Doug cried from his position, marching out in the middle of their formation and almost earning himself a kick in the face from Rachel.

She stumbled with the effort of avoiding that kick. "Ugh," she grunted, regaining her balance.

Colby caught her and exhaled roughly. "What, Doug? We were fine."

"Fine?" Doug repeated in his higher-pitched, offended tone. "*Fine* is not Andante, Colby Jack!"

"Oh boy," Rachel muttered. "You're in for it now, Cheesehead."

Colby snorted a laugh and nudged her.

"Rachel Ray, you are lagging in your jumps," Doug barked, snapping his fingers repeatedly. He came over to her, took her arm, and hauled her back to her mark. "You will never go anywhere, pumpernickel, if you can't do this gracefully. Now, I'll be the damsel, and you watch me. Colpepper, do your thing."

Rachel heaved a sigh and folded her arms, ignoring the almost gag-inducing stench of body odor, cheap cologne, and old cigarette smoke that was the essence of Doug. The man was a former Broadway and ballet dancer and had done some time on the ballroom scene as well, and he couldn't deal with the idea of being a has-been.

So now he was an "anything you can do, I can do better" type.

Such fun.

Doug went through Rachel's part, calling out the moves as he did them. "*Plié. Glissade. Battement. Soutinou, soutinou, jeté,* double *coupé* turn . . ."

This was ridiculous. Doug was doing the moves just fine, but Rachel definitely hadn't been lagging and definitely didn't need this demeaning demonstration.

"And ta-da!" Doug finished the motion on the floor, legs

sprawled, clinging to Colby's legs with more drama than Rachel ever did when they reached that point. "Not that difficult, lady. You also lack emotion. If the audience doesn't feel it, you're wasting everybody's time, and we'll return you to your place in the back row."

Rachel's eyes widened, and she raised her brows.

Colby stared at her in horror, clamping down on his lips hard.

"Right," Monica said slowly, walking across the stage. "Let's try the parallels one more time, and run through to the end. I think we're about done."

Rachel nodded and returned to the position at the beginning of the set.

Monica cleared her throat pointedly. "Doug. Give them some space."

Rachel glanced over to see Doug standing directly in the path of their parallels, eying Rachel with severity. The man sniffed once, then stomped over to stand next to Monica. "Okay, dancers. Five, six, seven, eight . . ."

They went through each of the moves, just as they had before, and finished the entire piece without interruption. It was smooth, accurate, and on time, exactly as it had been all of the other times they had done it, no matter what Doug had to say on the subject.

When it was over, Monica nodded her approval, smiling with an open palm on her cheek, just as she tended to do when she was truly pleased. "Lovely. Absolutely lovely."

Doug scoffed loudly but said nothing. His expression was enough.

Monica glanced at him, then smiled at Colby and Rachel. "If you guys don't mind stopping by and seeing Sara for some last-minute costume adjustments, that'd be great. Then you're free to go. We'll pick up tomorrow."

Rachel released an exhale and returned her director's smile. "Sounds good. Thanks, Mon." She turned and jogged down the stairs of the stage, grabbing her bag and turning out of the auditorium to move down the hall.

"Hey, Rach, wait up!"

Rachel paused and smiled at her partner, though her smile was a tired, loopy one. "Hurry. I'm going to fall over any minute."

Colby laughed as he reached her, walking in the same direction she was. "Well, as long as you do so gracefully and don't lag."

"Ugh," Rachel groaned, craning her neck. "I don't know what I did to irritate that man, but clearly I've done a great job."

"Clearly." Colby gave her a shrug and adjusted the strap of his bag on his shoulder. "Man, I hate this place."

Now *that* was a surprising statement, and Rachel gave him the sort of look that said so. "What?"

He returned her look. "You don't think I've been looking at other companies and auditioning wherever I can? This isn't the big time by any stretch, and I don't need to settle. Monica's fine, and the shows are too, but it's just the same old stuff. I like a challenge."

Rachel frowned to herself, turning that over. "Well, don't go anywhere too fast," she joked. "You know you're my favorite partner."

Colby snorted once. "You mean I'm the only one up to your talent. Honestly, you could dance anywhere."

"Except New York City," she retorted with a token level of snark before she could stop herself.

Her partner took her upper arm firmly, but not hard. "Rach, there's more places to make it than the Big Apple. Heck, there's even small companies in New York that would love you! Just think about it, okay?"

Think about it? Oh, she could think about it, and she had thought about it. She wanted nothing more than the chance to dance with a company that was going places, one that matched her passion and her tastes, one that challenged and excited her . . .

The problem was that she didn't know if she could bear to hope for that again. If she could endure the risk of failure again. If she could open up the reality of the dream again.

She just didn't know.

David rubbed his eyes and exhaled. He was so tired, and his body was telling him to go back home and go to bed. He'd had a light practice this morning, something to keep them loose after their late travel and games over the last few days, and they would be back to games tomorrow.

Normally he thrived on their almost-frantic schedule, and he had done since before Belltown.

But late-night phone calls with Rachel and overactive thoughts had done a fair job of distracting him from his usual ability to sleep on command.

Which was why he sat here in his truck in front of the Andante studio, slapping his cheeks and trying to get himself to not look sleep deprived.

And he was a little nervous.

He hadn't seen Rachel since their kiss in Belltown. They had talked and texted every day without fail, sometimes multiple times. But they hadn't physically been in the same place at the same time in over a week.

He wasn't sure how this was going to go.

But he couldn't sit in the truck forever, and he was dying to see Rachel.

A jolt of excitement lanced his gut and spurred him out

of the truck. He grinned to himself as he moved to the studio door and pulled it open. The entry was filled with pictures from past performances, and he focused on one in particular that was a close-up of Rachel in a pose that reminded him of his horrific yoga experience.

Only she looked incredible.

Magnificent.

Stunning.

How could he miss her so much that his teeth ached?

"Grizz?"

David jumped at hearing his name. He turned to see a trim woman with dark hair and dark eyes, dressed in black leggings and a gray cutoff sweatshirt, revealing toned abs and a diamond navel piercing. The curious tilt of her head and the messy bun on top of her head gave her a very youthful appearance. Did teenagers dance with Andante?

"That's me," he covered with a grin. "One and only."

"Oh, snap." She shook her head, hoisting the strap of her bag over her head so it would hang across her body. "Rach is going to buzz from head to toe."

He brightened at that. "You know Rachel?"

She sputtered loudly. "I know her. I'm Meghan Brock, best friend of your heart's desire."

David's grin spread, and he extended his hand. "Ah, I've heard of you. David McCarthy—call me Grizz."

Meghan took his hand, her smile turning suggestive. "I'll call you whatever you say, doll."

Sensing he was being played with, David laughed. "So Rachel's going to buzz, eh?"

"Considering the giggly look on her face every time she got a text from you?" Meghan quirked her brows repeatedly. "Oh yeah. Total buzz."

Why such a ridiculous statement would make him feel lighter than air and get his adrenaline pumping, he had no idea, but he started off towards the stage, as indicated by the signs.

His arm was suddenly grabbed. "Oh, no, you wait here, hunky. She's in her head right now. Rehearsal time, and no outsiders allowed. I'll check if it's safe and send her out if it is."

David raised a brow at her. "So I can't go watch?"

Meghan gave him a horrified look. "No! Not during tech week. Stress level at a twelve, dude. Like 'please send donuts, bring me caffeine' level."

"Ouch," he murmured in response, not quite understanding but not willing to ask for clarification. He did know what it was like in the days leading up to a big event, or a game or series in his case, and it did have a tendency to leave him constantly on the edge of nauseous. Somehow, he hadn't thought that it would be the same for Rachel in her world.

Why, he had no idea.

Idiot.

"So I should go?" he asked, frowning in thought.

Meghan groaned loudly. "No! Good friggin' crud, men are so dumb. Stay there. BRB." She whirled and pushed through the doors towards the stage, leaving David alone in the foyer with the pictures again.

He stroked his beard absently, wishing he had thought to bring something for her or to dress more nicely than faded jeans, a T-shirt, and a backwards cap. He had remembered deodorant and hadn't doused himself in cologne, so he could count that as a win.

But still.

He didn't know if he ever wanted to be completely comfortable where Rachel was concerned. It might benefit him to always want to impress her, to be on the edge of insecure, and so forth. Rachel could have anyone, and for some insane reason, she liked him.

Or didn't mind kissing him, at least.

Or . . .

Well, he didn't really know, which is what was driving him the most crazy.

And waiting wasn't helping.

The doors opened, and he turned towards them expectantly, only to see Meghan coming back out.

"Oof," she grunted with a wince, pressing a closed fist to her chest. "Such a sad face. There go my hopes and dreams." She grinned and winked. "Kidding, lover boy. She's on her way."

David nodded his thanks, smiling at her. Then his smile spread as he watched her prop herself against the currently empty ticket booth. "You're sticking around?"

Meghan widened her eyes and gestured grandly. "Um, yeah. Not missing this reunion. I'm a sucker for the romance. And I didn't tell Rach you were here."

"You didn't?" He gaped, anticipation skyrocketing.

"Nope. Just told her to hurry up, that I wanted food, and she said she was on her way." Meghan shrugged, her smile turning downright impish. "I'm so freaking excited, Grizz. You have no idea."

David was fairly certain he did have some idea, and a fairly clear one, but he wasn't about to contradict her.

The doors opened again, and with that came a gasp that seemed to make him do the same.

Slowly, he turned, and there stood Rachel, her bag slung over one shoulder, oversized pale-pink sweatshirt hanging lopsided on her, exposing one shoulder and leotard strap. She wasn't wearing makeup, and her hair was pulled back into a short ponytail, though some blond locks escaped it. Her trim legs were encased in leggings, her feet tucked into faded boat shoes that, strangely enough, had green shoelaces.

She looked amazing.

"Hi," he said stupidly, trying for a smile, which was difficult with his face feeling completely numb.

Rachel didn't say a word. She let her bag fall to the floor and started towards him, only breaking into a smile when she had almost reached him. "Hi yourself," she replied as she jumped into his waiting arms, wrapping her legs around him, clinging tightly.

David couldn't breathe as he enveloped her in his hold, burying his face into her shoulder, inhaling her fragrance. It didn't matter that she had just finished a workout; somehow she smelled of honey and something floral.

And she felt so incredible in his arms.

So perfect.

"I'm just gonna step out before this gets awkward . . ." Meghan said as she slipped back through the door Rachel had come out of.

He felt her nuzzling against his shoulder, and he chuckled. "You turning into a cat there?"

"You smell so freaking good," Rachel moaned, inhaling deeply as she did so. "I missed this so much."

He pulled back to give her a scolding look. "That's what you missed? Not my actual person?"

Rachel laced her hands behind his neck, grinning. "I could see you, I could hear you, I could text you. You still made me laugh and made me smile . . . but I couldn't smell you." Her fingers traced absent patterns against his neck. "Or touch you." Her eyes flicked down to his lips.

He leaned forward to kiss her before she could say the obvious, after which he would have kissed her anyway. She hummed against him, tugging him closer, then breaking off before either of them could get carried away.

David leaned his brow against hers, exhaling roughly.

"Well, I certainly missed all of you, babe. Every blessed inch." He rubbed her back slowly.

Rachel arched back and smirked playfully. "You had better, mister, if you're gonna call me *babe* like that."

"Doesn't bother you?" he asked, giving her hazel eyes a thorough look.

She shook her head. "Nope. I like it. Lots."

"Well, this is still precious and all kinds of hot," Meghan drawled as she reappeared, "but I'd rather not be here when parental guidance is suggested. And Your Royal Hotnesses are blocking the only viable exit."

Rachel dropped her head back and giggled wildly. "Oh, lands, Megs. My bad." She lowered her legs from David and patted his chest with a wink. "Rehearsal high plus hot guy back in town. You get it."

"Uh, totes get it," came the response. "Did you ice down?"

Rachel waved a dismissive hand. "I'll do it when I get home. I'm too hyped, don't want to cramp."

"Do I hear someone not taking care of her body?" David teased with a nudge to her side.

That earned him a dark look. "My legs are still shaking from repeated *saut de chats* and *coupé-chassé en tournants*. I can't ice right after that. I need some yoga first."

Oh *hell* no.

"Not you too," he groaned, rubbing his eyes. "No, no, no . . ."

The girls looked at him as if he'd sprouted a giraffe out of the top of his head. "Yoga is great for stretching and cooling down. Better than your basic baseball stretches, which I'm willing to bet you don't actually do even when you're supposed to."

David scowled, then had a rather brilliant, if cunning, idea. "Prove it."

"What?" she retorted, folding her arms, confusion an adorable shade on her. "Prove what?"

He shrugged a shoulder. "Prove to me that what you do is made better by that idiotic yoga I attempted."

Rachel just stared at him. "You want me to cite my resources?"

"Cute," he told her with a smile. "Teach would be so proud. But no, I want . . . I would like you to show me some of your moves."

"Moves?" she repeated. "Dance moves?"

"Well, I don't think he's talking Twister, chica," Meghan chimed in dryly. "Go on. Prove to the man that we know what we're talking about."

Rachel glanced at her friend. "Together?"

"Psht." Meghan held up a hand as if to stop her. "He does not want to look at me moving. Your show, babe. Have at."

"She says like it's a compliment," Rachel muttered. She sighed and moved to some open space. "Fine, I'll show you what I just finished doing." She slipped out of her shoes and craned her neck, pointing her toes and cracking her ankles.

"Careful," Meghan murmured as she folded her arms, though there was some distinct admiration in her tone.

Rachel nodded, then exhaled slowly. She started forward, toes pointed, did a sort of hop skip, then leaped into the air, her legs extending straight out, one in front and one behind. A full split in the air, and then she gracefully came back down to earth. She smiled up at him, shaking out her legs a little. "That's a *saut de chat.*"

"Impressive," David praised, unable to take his eyes off of her.

"Nobody jumps like Rach, I promise you that," Meghan assured him. "Best there is."

"Am not," Rachel protested, her cheeks turning pink.

Despite her argument, David suspected she really was. He had no proof of it, but he was fairly confident he was right.

"Next," Rachel went on, pressing her foot flat against the floor. Her front foot slid along the floor, her arm following the same motion. Then she snapped her legs together and turned, rotating twice without any difficulty whatsoever. She came out of the turn with ease and showed no hint of dizziness that he would have felt attempting the same. "Double *coupé* turn."

She went through more movements, giving him the names and making it look effortless. David didn't care what they were called, and he wouldn't have been able to remember anyway. What he did care about was that Rachel's dancing might have been the most beautiful thing he'd ever seen. She wasn't even doing a piece, just showing him a couple of moves, and he was in awe.

More than in awe, he was impressed, intimidated, and breathless all at once. He'd been teasing her about yoga, but suddenly nothing that Rachel could do or did do relating to her dancing was in any way ridiculous or something to joke about.

Somehow, she combined art and athleticism into one, creating something glorious that was a privilege to witness.

"Ow!" Rachel suddenly yelped, gripping her left foot. "Cramp, cramp, ouch . . ."

Meghan came over and waved Rachel down to the floor, then took her foot and stretched it, rubbing right in the sole. "Take it easy, girl. Demonstration time is over."

"I'm an idiot," Rachel groaned, putting a hand to her brow. "It's show week, and I thought it was a good idea to show off just after a tough rehearsal. My arches have been sore for days, and I just had to push it. It's going to happen in the show, I know it. I'm going to screw it all up and not hit my jumps, and then Doug is going to be right. Designated back row for me."

"What?" David looked at Meghan in bewilderment.

Meghan rolled her eyes. "Hello, this is your regular thought process. I can't come to the phone right now, so leave a message while overthinking takes over."

Rachel tried to slap her friend's hand, then grunted in pain as Meghan hit an apparently good spot. "Overthinking is the number-one skill on my resume." She looked over at David and smiled gently. "You should have seen me after that night in Belltown."

David returned her smile slowly. "I'm not an overthinker, babe. But after that night, I became one too."

Chapter 9

THE ROOM WAS full, but that wasn't saying much. It was a small auditorium, though the stage was a decent enough size. It would have to be to house the entire company of dancers on a regular basis, but David had thought there would be more seats.

That ought to have been the case for a company that had dancers of Rachel's caliber in their ranks. Tons and tons of seats, all of them full every night.

But here he was, seated in the middle of a row of markedly uncomfortable theater seats, wearing a dress shirt, no tie, waiting to watch Rachel perform.

There couldn't be more than a hundred people in here, and that was being generous. They spanned the dress code as well, some wearing jeans and T-shirts while others chose the more formal apparel better suited for a gala.

Thankfully, David fell somewhere in the middle. He had checked with Rachel repeatedly, not wanting to embarrass her by wearing the wrong thing. There would be plenty else he would say or do that would take care of that for him, but if he could avoid doing so at the beginning of this relationship, it gave him more time to leave a good impression.

He hadn't even been noticed this evening as Grizz McCarthy, and that seemed, somehow, a small victory. He wouldn't know what to say if people asked what he was doing at the show or about his relationship with Rachel, if that came out. They weren't officially anything, except crazy about each other. They hadn't put names on it or used any particular terms.

They just . . . were.

He wasn't comfortable with such a vague sentiment, but there was nothing he could do about that at the moment. If he was discovered, he would have to say that he was watching an old friend perform. After all, that was a true statement, in every sense of the word.

It lacked a certain depth and didn't take into account his intense attraction towards her or the fascination he suddenly had with her lips, but it would suffice.

For now.

Music suddenly filled the air, and David looked up to the stage expectantly. The curtains pulled back with the same sort of jerky movements one saw in high school plays and musicals, and there was no one on the stage. Only blue lights that sporadically cut into the sea of blackness that was the rest of the space.

Then, out of the shadows, dancers began to appear, and the sound of rain could be heard over the speakers. It took him a minute, but eventually he could see the movements of the dancers, their tumbling, twirling, and tossing each other across the stage, all illustrated various aspects of a storm. Some women mimicked splashing into puddles while others seemed to be imitating raindrops themselves.

Identities were completely obscured by the lack of true lighting, so he had no idea of knowing if Rachel was currently on the stage. So far there had not been anything from any performer that even remotely expressed any individuality. All very uniform and cohesive, and kind of hypnotizing, he had to admit. The more he watched it, the more fascinated he became.

Suddenly, one dancer in the back of the group was tossed into the air, flipping end over end, then opening up into a full split just as a spotlight winked on her.

He knew who it was at once.

Rachel.

The light winked off again as she relaxed into a graceful fall and was caught by other dancers.

David shook his head, breathless with the sheer acrobatic feat she had just accomplished.

Two others did something similar, though their height did not match Rachel's, nor did their agility.

He felt a proud burst of pleasure at that.

The sounds of the storm began to fade, and the occasional member of the company began to trickle off of the stage, the tumbling and movement slowing and growing less intense. Soon, there were only three members on the stage, and one of them began running, then leaped into the air, seeming to soar like a bird, the spotlight winking on her again just before she vanished into the edge of the stage, her descent completely obscured.

How could Rachel possibly get that high into the air without the help of another person or a trampoline of some kind?

The sheer physics of it astounded him, and he could only sit back in his seat, staring at the now-vacant and dark stage while applause roared around him. He belatedly joined in, but there was no ridding himself of the sense that his appreciation was only just beginning.

Andante was clearly full of very talented people, and it

wasn't difficult to identify his favorite pieces in the show. A few had been so completely abstract that David wasn't sure he understood the point of it, let alone any sort of theme. The talent was undeniable, but if he was left with a confused expression on his face, talent alone wasn't enough.

What did surprise him was a solo piece by Meghan that was almost entirely ballet, pointe shoes and all. It reminded him of attending his cousin Josie's performance of the Nutcracker when he was eleven, though he'd hated that particular rite of passage in his childhood. Meghan was far more talented, and her almost-frantic personality could not have been more perfectly contained than in her performance. Somehow, she was filled with energy that kept all eyes on her even without her impressive abilities.

He recognized some of the moves that Rachel had showed him the other day, though their names were blending with various Italian menu items, making the whole thing completely nonsensical.

Meghan had far more grace than he had anticipated, and he found himself smiling as he watched her spin, jump, arch . . . She needed no partner on the stage, and for some reason, that seemed significant. David would have to compliment her and ask her for the information he needed.

For example, why was she in all black when the music was so light?

It wasn't significant, but he was sure Meghan would have an answer, and chances were, it would be an entertaining one.

A series of sleepy numbers he wouldn't remember passed, and Rachel was in one or two but had no real significance to the piece at hand. David hated to say it, but he was getting bored with some of them. Rachel was better than this.

He didn't know how he knew that, but he did.

He was no judge of dancing talent, far from it, but even Meghan was better than this, and she'd said Rachel was the best.

He was willing to take her word for it.

At last, Rachel returned to the stage with a tall, slender, but built man he had seen in a few of the other performances.

From the very first pose, David didn't particularly care for the guy.

Once the dancing began, he didn't like him at all, and he had to grip the armrests of his chair.

The dance between them was magnificent, but David was frozen watching it. The way Rachel moved eclipsed any emotion and went straight to his heart, lighting it up like the Chicago skyline. She moved against her partner, with him, with a sort of fluidity he had only ever seen in water and art. She was lifted into the air, then somehow tumbled end over end down her partner's back.

It was as if there were a romance between them, but it was more than the gazes they shared. Everything about the movement and motion spoke to an intensity that could only be felt, and he marveled that such a thing could be captured on the stage in this way. David watched as the pair of them mirrored each other, doing the exact same motions at the exact same time in the same pattern, until Rachel spun towards her partner, then sank to the ground and was swung gracefully around.

He had only ever seen things like this in ice skating on TV, but this was without the gliding assistance of a blade on ice. This was just two people on a stage without shoes or props, but the emotion was the same. Perhaps more, even.

Not even because it was Rachel, though there was some significant impact to him because of that fact.

This was quite simply beautiful.

And he was insanely jealous of the man up there sharing it with her.

The dance slowed as Rachel was lowered to the floor, her partner lowering with her, then cupping her cheek as the music faded and the lights dimmed.

Breathless, David joined in the applause, shaking his head yet again.

He'd never known that Rachel, or anyone, could make him feel so much with a dance. That it could move him in such a way. He'd been impressed watching her before, aware of her skills and her strength, but putting it all together when she was on display, in this atmosphere, defied anything he'd felt in his life.

He was so insanely proud of her, and he wanted to rush the stage and sweep her up. He wanted to carry her on his shoulders and declare to the whole world that she was his. He wanted to shoot off fireworks and strike up a band of sorts. Anything to scream victory and triumph.

But that was his world, not hers. In baseball they could have the fanfare and the storming of the field, the music and the parades.

In dancing?

What did one do?

The audience began to get up from their seats and depart, and David, belatedly, did the same. He slipped out of the auditorium, pulling his phone out quickly, dialing one of the few numbers he knew by heart.

It only rang twice.

"Mamma Sal, hi," he said with a quick smile she wouldn't see. "I need your help."

Rachel had never heard of a princess in a tower having

her prince's love declaration set to the sound of techno dance music, but there were worse things.

If only her prince would get on with it.

She was right here, and he could tell her how he felt before riding away with her into the sunset . . .

The music increased in volume and clarity just as he opened his mouth, and Rachel sighed in disappointment.

Then she pried one eye open and looked over at the offending phone on her nightstand, blaring the same annoying strains of a once-entertaining song.

She lifted her head and looked at the clock across the room and groaned. This was the third or fourth time she had woken up since 5:42 this morning, and the dreams had only gotten weirder between clock checks.

The techno blared again, and her right hand flailed for the phone.

Her thumb automatically hit the button without looking, and she brought the phone to her ear. "Hello?"

"Whoa," David's voice exclaimed. "Who drugged you?"

Rachel laughed, mostly into her pillow, warmth spreading through her limbs. "Ha ha. It's the weekend, and I finally don't have a show or rehearsal. And I don't have work."

"And all of this means that you sound like the dead?"

"It means," Rachel grunted, turning over onto her back, "that I am in bed."

There was a beat of silence from the other end of the line, and she imagined him checking the clock. "Still?" he finally said. "It's 9:17. This is late for you."

"It's really very simple, babe," she told him with a yawn. "If I get out of bed, the day starts. If the day starts, I have to think and do things. If I have to think and do things, I get stressed. If I get stressed, things don't get done, and I wallow in failure. If I wallow in failure, the day is a loss. Ergo, I am staying in bed for my own health and safety."

"Wow," he replied slowly, drawing the word out unnecessarily.

"What?" Rachel shot back, grinning up at her ceiling.

David's chuckle did ticklish things to the soles of her feet, and she shifted restlessly in her sheets. "You overthink before you even get up," he told her. "That's amazing. I'll be there in five minutes with donuts and chocolate milk."

Rachel shot straight up in bed, one hand going to her wildly disheveled hair. "Breakfast in bed?"

"Not quite. You have to get out of bed to let me in."

"I sense a trap," she mused with a frown.

"How badly do you want the donuts?" David asked.

Silence stretched between them, the only sound the very faint sound of David's turn signal coming through the phone. Then Rachel heaved a sigh and scowled at nothing. "The bill for my therapy is going to you."

"Okay," he replied without concern. "Be there in four."

David hung up first, and Rachel stared straight ahead without blinking.

Four minutes.

Four minutes to go from groggy sea witch to stunning belle of the ball.

"Blessed Delilah, preserve us," Rachel groaned as she rolled off of her bed and stumbled into the bathroom. Four minutes wasn't enough time for a shower, for much in the way of real clothing, or for actually putting her face together.

But it was enough time to go from skanky sleep shorts to nice sweats and to take her breath from deadly to minty fresh.

It was enough time for a brush to attack her hair, for a shirt that didn't smell like drool and body odor to slide over powdery fresh armpits, and for eyeliner and mascara.

Wasn't time for much more than that, but at least now she didn't look like a zombie.

Oh, Lord, her apartment . . .

With a shriek of dismay, she tore from the bathroom to the front of the place, grabbing blankets and socks from the floor, grateful that she'd at least taken the trash out yesterday. And that she hadn't gone for the Chinese takeout she'd been craving in order to get home in time to see the end of David's game.

They'd won, and he'd been fantastic, throwing out a guy on second with a blazing throw she had whooped over as the game ended. Then she'd practically collapsed into bed, and now she was running around trying to make it look like she had some semblance of cleanliness in her life.

She really should have tried to go for matching furniture. It looked like a poor, starving college student lived here.

Not that she was rolling in the money and successfully leading an adult life, but still.

Nothing about this place was going to impress David.

She tossed the blankets and socks into the closet that was her laundry room, shut the door, and turned to face the front door as a knock sounded on it.

A rush of air left Rachel's lungs as she recalled that, just on the other side, would be David McCarthy who had come expressly to see her on his off day.

And he would have donuts.

Who in their right mind would refuse something like that?

Rachel hurried to the door, already grinning. Flinging open the door, she fixed her expression into one of seductive derision. "You bring my donuts?"

David gave her a slow look up and down, one side of his mouth curving into a smile that made her knees buckle. He held up the promised bag of donuts and tilted his head. "As promised. You going to let me in, gorgeous?"

Fighting back a shiver, she pushed the door open farther in invitation. "Come on in."

He took a step forward, then grinned at her when she did not move. "I see, I have to get past you?"

She nodded. "That's right."

"Hmm." He stepped closer and leaned down to caress her lips with his own, keeping far enough away that nothing else touched her.

Heat raced through her from the simple connection of their lips, but the lack of other contact created a shocking breeze that was almost icy. She shivered and edged closer to the furnace that was David, only for him to break their connection and step back.

His smile was rueful, and he waved the bag of donuts before her eyes. "Donuts first."

Rachel pouted. "Rude."

David clicked his tongue and lowered the bag. "Then I guess you really don't want the chocolate milk, or to taste the maple bar that is still warm from the bakery."

She snatched the bag from him and whirled for her couch. "You're right. Donuts first. Hunger before kisses."

She heard him laugh as he followed, shutting her door behind him. "Nice place, Rach. Comfortable, cozy, and convenient."

Rachel looked up from her spot, pausing her rummaging in the bag to glance around. Her place was sparse, as far as decor and furniture went, and she had more blankets to her name than chairs to sit in. Her movie collection, proudly on display, was this close to pathetic, and if anyone looked in her cupboards, they would have been shocked by the mismatched hodgepodge that was her dishes.

She couldn't argue the comfortable; there was nothing ostentatious or intimidating about the place. She would absolutely consider her place cozy; the blankets alone made it so.

But convenient? She wasn't in the best part of Pittsburgh, and she was not in the worst. Parking was miserable, there were a dozen one-way streets to get lost on finding it, and the nearest ice cream place was just far enough away that it required serious consideration on whether to venture out on foot or waste the gas on the one-way streets and traffic of taking the car.

"Convenient?" she repeated with a laugh, pulling out a napkin and setting it on the coffee table. "To what? It's in a crazy annoying spot."

David smiled at her as he removed his tennis shoes, and she noticed, for the first time, that he was in sweats too. His T-shirt fit better than hers did, which her eyes very much appreciated, and she suddenly had a brief vision of spending regular Saturday mornings going from bed to couch, sweats on, donuts in hand, and watching the highlights of David's games the night before. Just the two of them together, snuggling lazily and dozing on each other in a pleasant weekend lethargy.

Rachel bit her lip with sudden longing.

"Convenient," David said again as he came to sit down beside her, one arm going to the back of the couch, "because it is less than ten minutes from my place, just a few blocks from Eddie's, and on the way to the ballpark. Very, very convenient." He leaned close again, his intentions clear.

Rachel raised a warm maple bar and took a large bite of it before he could do anything his eyes had promised. "Mmm," she hummed with a dramatic rolling-back of her eyes. "Oh my gosh, this is glorious."

He scowled darkly. "And you said I was rude."

She waved her donut at him. "Donuts. You have the drinks?"

David sighed and pulled bottles of chocolate milk out of the pockets of his sweats. "Only the good stuff." He opened the chocolate milk for them both and handed one to her.

She clinked it against his and downed two gulps before setting her drink down on the table. "I hope you weren't expecting me to be more ladylike when you came over," she managed as she took another bite. "Manners wait for no donut."

"I'm fairly certain I've never found you more attractive," he returned, taking a bite out of a bear claw the size of her face. He tossed back his chocolate milk, his Adam's apple bobbing with several swallows, glimpses of his tattoo dancing with the edge of his sleeve with tantalizing motions.

Oddly enough, she had never found *him* more attractive, and her lips tingled with the urge to kiss him right where her attention was fixed.

David sighed and set his chocolate milk down, then leaned back against the couch, patting the cushion. "Come here."

Needing no further encouragement, Rachel nestled up against him, exhaling with delight when his hand settled on her upper arm, stroking gently. "Mmm, this is nice."

He kissed the top of her head. "This is perfect. I think it's a new tradition when I'm in town."

"All in favor?" Rachel raised her hand and chuckled when David did too. "Motion carries."

"Good."

They sat in silence for a moment, munching on their donuts comfortably. "So," David eventually said, "got any plans today?"

Rachel shrugged against him. "Just going to your game. Why?"

"What would you say to . . . going on a date with me?" he

asked, his fingers still tracing patterns against her arm. "A real one. I could pretend to be your boyfriend this time; it could be fun."

"Or . . ." Rachel said slowly, lifting her head and pursing her lips in thought, "you could really be my boyfriend and not pretend anything. That would be even more fun." She turned and met his eyes squarely, her heart pounding with thunderous anxiety.

David stared at her, his brilliant blue eyes wide, and it was all she could do to maintain eye contact.

Please say yes. Please, please say yes . . .

David's free hand rose to cup her cheek, his thumb stroking her skin gently. Then he leaned forward and kissed her with a fierceness that stopped her heart and curled her toes. She matched him, gripping his T-shirt in hand, her fingers brushing the rock-hard abs beneath the fabric.

The kiss was as short as it was intense, and Rachel's head swam as she dropped her brow to rest against his chin. "David . . ."

He shifted slightly to kiss her brow. "Yes, baby?"

She laughed softly and raised her head, sighing. "Can I wear your jersey to the game?" She quirked her brows teasingly.

David grinned swiftly, then tapped her nose. "Hold that thought." He got up and went back to the front door, opening it and reaching for something he had apparently left out in the hall.

"What?" Rachel demanded, sitting forward on the couch to see. "What's there?"

He turned and held out a bouquet of at least a dozen yellow roses and a sheepish grin on his handsome face. "I didn't know I was supposed to bring flowers the other night to your show. You blew me away, and I haven't been able to get you out of my mind ever since. Belated though these are, will you accept them as a gesture of admiration, of congratulations, and of how ridiculously proud of you I am?"

Lord have mercy.

Rachel slowly got up from the couch and came over to him. She took the flowers from his arms, smelled them just for a moment, then set them down on the couch and threw her arms around her boyfriend's neck, kissing him hard, going up on her toes. His hands encased her waist, keeping her close, and his beard rubbed against the skin of her jaw and cheeks with a ticklish abrasiveness that heightened every sensation within her.

"I accept," Rachel whispered deliriously against David's delicious onslaught. "I very much accept."

CHAPTER 10

"Second!"

Dragged from his errant thoughts of Rachel, David shook himself and returned to the activity around him. He watched as Rodriguez scooped up the bunt and launched to second during the practice drill, overthrowing enough that AD had to jump to catch it, barely able to tag the base before firing the ball to first.

He winced at that. Roddy wasn't going to be happy with that, but he'd had a good practice regardless. He was a fantastic catcher, and his only hang-up was that he was young. He'd only been up from the minors for a year, and he had yet to really make his mark. In that sense, Pittsburgh would be a great team for him. Time to grow and room to develop without much by way of pressure.

Of course, having David on the team would also ensure that Roddy didn't get much attention.

Not that Roddy would blame David for it. No one could help the Six Pack fever, and David had worked hard to be as good as he was.

If only he had a team to match it.

He stepped up for his turn, crouching down into position.

Coach bunted the ball, and it veered left. "First!"

David dashed forward, thinking quickly as he faced third. He pivoted on his right foot, his left sliding in the dirt to stabilize him as he threw the ball hard towards first base. Something pulled tight in his left knee, and he grunted softly, watching as the ball soared right into Lima's glove with a perfect sounding clap.

"Atta boy, Grizz!" Lima called, pointing his glove at him.

David nodded and straightened, walking back to home plate, the back of his left knee roaring at him, but not enough to limp.

He'd need to watch that. His knees were his lifeblood in this game, and if there was anything going on there . . .

"Infield drills," Coach told them all suddenly. He turned to look at David and Roddy. "You guys can hop in if you want, or join the outfielders. Unless you want to jump over to the bullpen, but they're almost done."

David and Roddy shared looks and shrugged. "I'll go infield," Roddy offered. "Looks like I could use the help."

"And I was just thinking I could use some pop-up work," David added with a smile. "Always a nice refresher."

They tagged each other's gloves and jogged to the separate ends of the field. The outfielders cheered when David joined them, acting as though an outfield versus infield game of dodgeball was about to start. He shook his head, rolling his eyes. The outfielders were great guys, and they had all been with him last year for the World Series run, but they were also the biggest goofballs he knew outside of the Six Pack.

And the bullpen.

There was just something wrong with the pitchers on this team, and no one could explain it.

Cowboy crouched in preparation for the first pop-up and began whistling the fight song for Albany State, arguably Belltown's greatest rival, and his Alma Mater.

"Ugh, what is that awful sound?" David groaned with a wince, covering his ears. "T-Money, shoot that tone-deaf bird out of the sky, would you?"

Obediently, T-Money aimed his imaginary rifle into the sky, cocked it, and made the sound of firing it.

"Nice shot," David complimented, still covering his ears.

"That's how we do things in Texas," his teammate drawled, shouldering the pretend rifle with a nod.

"You missed," Cowboy replied without a hint of twang. It was the biggest team joke, having the actual Texas cowboy without the matching name and the total New York city slicker who just loved cowboy hats getting it instead.

"O Canada . . ." Bert began to sing out of nowhere.

The others turned to him. "Shut up, Bert," they said as one.

Bert laughed and held up his hands. "Eh, just trying to make the peace, boys."

"You would, you crazy Canadian," T-Money said, shaking his head.

Cowboy ran for the pop-up, catching it neatly and whooping as he threw it to Coach Lee in the infield. "Match that one, boys."

"Gladly." T-Money exhaled twice shortly, ready for the next ball. He sprinted off to his left and made an unnecessary leaping catch, whirling and belting out a loud, "Ha!" to the rest.

"No pressure," David grunted as he stepped forward.

Bert patted his back once. "No worries, Grizz. No one expects you to do that."

"Oh no?" He sprang ahead as the ball popped up, his eyes

trained on it. He mentally cursed, as he had gone too far, and began to backpedal quickly, his knee squealing in protest. He opened his mitt, reaching above his head and falling back, catching the ball as he did so just before hitting the ground with a whoosh of discomfort.

"Whoa!" the outfield cheered, applauding with enthusiasm. "Atta boy, Grizzy!"

The infield roared with the indignity of missing an apparently spectacular play.

It felt more awkward than anything else, and David shook his head as he clambered up. He didn't have another one of those in him, and he wasn't sure he should continue the drill at all. There was something about his knee that he didn't trust, and with the series against Dallas in a few days, he didn't dare push it.

"That's it for me," he said with a wave.

Bert sobered at once. "Grizzy, you good?"

He waved off the concern with a scoffing sound. "Oh yeah. Just don't wanna make you guys look bad, and I gotta ice my moneymakers."

"You ice your beard?" Cowboy asked with a teasing grin.

David stroked his beard at once. "Makes it grow thick and luscious. You should try it. Maybe then you'd look older than twelve."

Cowboy winced with the jab as the others laughed.

David jogged carefully to the dugout, getting a wave of acknowledgement from Coach before he removed his gear and made his way to the training room just outside of the clubhouse.

Sam was already inside getting things ready for post-practice treatments, and he smiled in surprise when he saw David. "Grizzy, you're in early. You okay?"

"Not sure, man," David admitted as he came over to him.

"Tweaked something in the back of my knee on a wonky catch. Not too bad, but enough that I didn't want to push it."

Sam was immediately all business and gestured for him to hop onto a table. He felt where David indicated and had him move his knee through various motions, asking that he tense his muscles in certain positions, push against him, and do other things that David didn't understand but complied with. He'd worked with athletic trainers and doctors enough to know that they had a reason for everything they asked, even if it wasn't obvious.

"Guessing it's the hamstrings," Sam told him as he lowered David's leg back down to the table. "Just a slight strain though. Everything feels good, your strength and motion is good, and nothing's giving where it shouldn't. Let's throw some ice and electric stimulation on it, and I want you stretching tonight and icing again before bed. Check in before practice in the morning, and we'll see how you are."

David nodded obediently and hopped off the table to shuck his pants off, leaving him in his compression shorts beneath, making it easier for treatment than keeping his pant leg hiked up. He got back up onto the table and lay on his stomach, grabbing his cell phone as he waited for Sam to return with the ice.

The Six Pack were texting again, and he scrolled quickly to catch up.

Big Dawg: Did y'all see me on the highlight reel this morning? Booyah!

Steal: They ran the Not Top Ten plays already? Wow.

Big Dawg: Haha

Axe: Was that when you guys danced in the dugout? I know it wasn't something you did ON the field.

Skeeter: Did you break a bat on that foul ball? That would be a highlight.

David shook his head with a laugh and checked the other message, this time from Rachel.

Rachel: Hey hot stuff. Work sucks today. Make me smile?

That made him sigh in both amusement and concern. He understood Rachel working at the dentist office to pay her bills and give her some stability, but the idiotic drama and borderline bullying surrounding her at that office took too much energy out of her. She wasn't even at the center of it all, skirting around most of it and keeping her head down, but she couldn't avoid it completely. She had been so tired when she finished her workday lately, and he could see the strain on her face.

Make her smile, she asked.

He made a face, considering just how he could do that.

His phone rang before he could decide on anything and he answered it quickly. "Mom? Hey."

"Hey, sweetheart," came the cheerful, yet oddly emotional voice of his mother. "Is this a good time?"

"Sure," he said slowly as Sam returned and began setting the treatment up on his leg. "Everything okay?"

His mom cleared her throat once. "Question. What are you doing next weekend?"

David thought quickly. "We're playing Miami for a few days. Why? What's up?"

"Do you think you could get out of going?" she asked, ignoring his inquiry.

He raised up on one elbow. "If it's a good reason, yeah. Rodriguez is due for a few games, and I just came off of a decent rotation. Coach Barker will need a reason, though, Mom."

"Oh, I have one." There was a long pause. "Clint's coming home."

David stilled, barely breathing as his leg began to twitch

with the electric stimulation treatment kicking on in it. "Is he okay?"

He would swear he could hear his mom's eager nod. "Yes. They're sending his unit home earlier than planned. He's done, David. He's coming home to stay!"

David's hand flew to his eyes in relief, then he laughed with the weight of it. "Mom, that's amazing! Of course I'll be there. Coach shouldn't have a problem with this."

"I didn't think so," came the now completely emotional reply. "And if he did, I'd just put in a call to Judy."

"Mom!" He chuckled again. "You can't sic Judy on Coach just to get your way!"

"Why not? She's his wife, and nobody messes with her!"

David put his head down on the treatment table, snickering. Then he sobered as an idea struck him. "Hey Mom . . . what would you say to my bringing my girlfriend with me? Would that be okay with you? Would Clint mind?"

"Seeing Rachel?" She laughed in what sounded like genuine delight. "Of course not! We'd love to have her! I'll make up the guest room!"

He pulled his phone back and stared at it before bringing it back to his ear. "How did you know I'm dating Rachel?"

"Oh, honey," came the very motherly reply. "Sally and I have been talking about it for weeks now. Some children actually tell their mothers about their love lives."

"Sorry I'm not that chatty," he shot back with an embarrassed smile. "I'll talk with Coach and check with Rach. I'll let you know the details, okay?"

"Okey-dokey. Can't wait to see you!"

"You too, Mom. Love you. Bye."

He hung up the phone and put his head back down, his mind spinning. Having Clint back home would be amazing. Bringing Rachel with him to see his family in an official capacity . . .

He returned his attention to his phone and began to type out a message.

Hey gorgeous. How does a trip to Chicago next weekend sound? I can promise great pizza, perfect hot dogs, and a homemade meal or two, courtesy of one Aubrey McCarthy.

He saw the three dots of a forthcoming reply, the vibrations of his heartbeat rippling across the surface of the treatment table beneath him.

Rachel: Smiling is happening. It's a date. Think we can catch a baseball game? Huge Spades fan over here.

David laughed louder than he meant to, and he texted back a quick reply, shaking his head.

He was still falling for this woman, and he was falling hard.

Dark-thirty flights were not Rachel's friend.

It wasn't that bad when she had a big, strong, remarkably comfortable boyfriend to snuggle up against and doze on for the duration of it. But considering she'd had to get up a full ninety minutes before he came to pick her up so that she could make herself presentable, she was beyond exhausted.

She looked great, but it was entirely possible that all of her pristine work would be smeared from her napping. Still, she'd brought stuff to touch up as needed when they landed in Chicago, and David wouldn't mind.

He had shown up in jeans and a T-shirt, with a Belltown jacket that he'd given her to wear as a blanket on the plane. And, true to form, he'd worn a Belltown cap, which was still on his head, tilted back as it was against the headrest.

David slept with his mouth open, and while he didn't quite snore, his sleeping exhales did make a certain amount of noise. She enjoyed the sound of it as they rumbled through his chest and into her. They'd raised the armrest between them so that there was no obstacle separating them, and he'd draped his arm around her comfortably as she had practically burrowed into his side.

She yawned and pried her eyes open, glancing out of the window. The flight was only an hour and half, and she wasn't sure how long she'd slept. She didn't remember the plane taking off or the flight attendants bringing drinks around, and she had no idea how soon they would land.

All she knew was that she ought to have been terrified at the prospect of spending an entire weekend with her boy-friend's family.

But she wasn't.

She'd known the McCarthys for years. Not all of them, granted, but she had certainly seen them enough in Belltown to be comfortable with Ed and Aubrey, and even Clint, though it had been a bit since she had seen him. The only qualm she had about the whole thing was that she had never been around them while she was in a relationship with David. While she freely kissed David. While she held his hand without even thinking about it.

She was ready for teasing; that would come with being around the McCarthys, dating David or not. But they could look at her in a new light now and somehow not find her good enough.

They'd never say so, but . . .

"Are you tired or are you overthinking?"

Rachel propped her chin on David's chest and looked up at him. "Yes."

He chuckled, eyes still closed, his arm pulling her closer to him. "Figures."

"How did you know?" she murmured as she slid an arm across his torso.

One side of his mouth curved. "You tensed in my arms. What are you overthinking about?"

"Being your girlfriend," she admitted, drumming her fingers against his side.

He cracked an eye open. "Second thoughts?"

She rolled her eyes and lightly whacked him. "No, dummy. Just thinking about being your girlfriend in front of your family."

His other eye opened, and he turned his face more fully towards her. "Babe, there's no list of requirements. You don't have any lines, and there's no choreography to remember. I haven't had a girlfriend in so long, I'm pretty sure they're more likely to try to impress you so you don't run away screaming."

The idea made her grin. "Are they going to shower me with gifts and buy my favorite things and cook my favorite meals?"

"Probably," he told her without any hint of teasing. "Mom said she was going to make up the guest room for you, and it wouldn't surprise me if she left chocolate mints on your pillow with a fresh copy of the newest book from your favorite author ready for you."

"How would she know my favorite author?" Rachel asked with a laugh. "You don't even know that."

He ran his fingers gently up her spine and back down again, making a face. "She's been talking to your mom."

Rachel winced loudly. "Oh boy. Think Skeeter knows about us?"

David shook his head very firmly. "Nope."

"So sure, are you?"

"I am." He quirked his brows, smiling at her. "Your mom told me she wouldn't tell."

Rachel gaped. "When did she tell you that?"

"Oh, back in Belltown," he replied, shrugging as his hand continued to move along her back. "She and I had a real heart-to-heart in the kitchen the night before you came. I was anxious about how I felt about you, and what to do about it."

"I'm afraid to ask," Rachel muttered, her face warming as she pictured David sitting up with her mom in the middle of the night to talk about her. It was cute and unsettling and tender all at the same time.

He kissed her brow very gently. "Don't be. Your mom is Team Grachel, so it's all good."

She buried her face in his chest with a snort of laughter. "Don't call us that ever again. Oh my gosh, that's horrible."

"I like it," he protested. "I'm making T-shirts."

"I'll burn them."

"Then I'll rent a banner for Cole to fly behind the jet."

"I'll date Cole for real."

"Pretty sure you'd have a hard time making that happen. He's pretty whipped."

Rachel groaned and shook her head against David, sighing. "You always have an answer for everything, don't you, David McCarthy?"

"Not even close," he assured her, adjusting his jacket on her. "I'm just a fan of us, and you're not changing that."

She peered up at him again, flashing a sleepy smile. "Me too. We're pretty fabulous."

He kissed her again, playing with her lips leisurely. "The best."

A soft dinging sound met their ears.

"Ladies and gentlemen, the captain has turned on the fasten seatbelt sign as we begin our initial descent into the Chicago area. At this time, we ask that you return your seats to your full, upright positions and put your tray tables up. We also ask that you put away any large electronic devices you may have pulled out during the flight . . ."

The rest of the message faded in Rachel's ears as she focused on the view out of the window, the light of the approaching dawn barely highlighting the land beneath them. "Already? Wow."

David was looking out of the window, too, but he didn't respond.

She glanced up at him, curious by the intense yet somehow whimsical expression he wore as he stared. "David?"

He shook himself out of his thoughts and looked down at her. "What?"

Rachel touched his chin, her fingers absently brushing through his beard. "Where were you then?"

He smiled gently at her, then indicated the window with his head. "I love the rainbow sky in the morning."

"The what now?" she asked, her brow furrowing.

David laughed and pointed at the window, but at the sky almost behind them. "When I'm on an early morning flight. If you look towards the east, just before sunrise, there's an actual rainbow across the horizon." He tapped the window twice. "I don't know why, but I've always loved that."

Rachel looked and smiled as she saw what he was talking about, and her heart buzzed with affection and delight. She gave him a wry look. "My word, Grizz McCarthy. You're a romantic."

He brought a finger to his lips. "Shh. Don't tell."

"Your secret's safe with me," she promised, arching up to kiss him very softly.

"I know it is," he whispered with a gentle stroke of her cheek.

Rachel heaved a dramatic sigh that made him roll his eyes and laugh. She pushed up from him, shrugging off his jacket and giving it back to him. "You're buying me breakfast, right?"

"I bought breakfast last time."

She scoffed and threw a disbelieving look at him. "Of the two of us, which one is the wealthy professional athlete?"

He fake coughed in dismay. "And this means it is my financial responsibility to feed you?"

"Well, yeah!" She nodded as if that should have been obvious. "It's in the boyfriend code."

His eyes narrowed at her. "What if neither of us pays for overpriced airport food, and we let my mother ask us if we've had breakfast, and when we say no, she'll get it for us?"

Rachel smiled slowly at him and nodded once. "You're a very devious man, David McCarthy. I like the way you think."

David took her hand and laced their fingers, quirking a brow. "What am I thinking now, Rachel?"

She laughed once. "That one's easy, babe." She leaned forward and kissed him until the flight attendant apologetically made them pull their seats back up.

CHAPTER 11

"NO, NO, ABSOLUTELY not."

"This isn't a debate. It's happening."

"Clint doesn't want to do this. Clint is exhausted, he's just come back from overseas, he's got jet lag."

"Clint feels fine, thank you very much. Clint is just happy to be here."

"Why is Clint speaking in third person?"

"Clint does what he wants."

David rolled his eyes at his brother, who had only been at the family house for two hours and was already up to his old tricks. He would be lying if he said that he hadn't teared up at seeing Clint coming towards them at the base earlier or that he hadn't hugged him more tightly or for a longer period than usual. He would freely admit that Clint looked older than he had when he'd left, that his brother looked stronger and trimmer and could actually pull off the completely clean-shaven, buzzed-haircut look without difficulty.

But Clint was, above and below all else, his little brother.

Annoying him was in his blood.

"Ugh, whatever, weirdo," their cousin Josie groaned as

she shoved off of the couch she had been sharing with him and slapped Clint's thigh hard, making him cry out in outrage. "I'm going to go recruit some others. We've got time before dinner, so we might as well make the most of it." She turned to Rachel with her usual infectious smile. "Wanna come? I may need you for the curiosity factor."

Rachel's eyes widened, and she looked at David, startled. "The what?"

David chuckled easily. "She means that if you're with her, the relatives just might say yes so they can spend more time with you to size you up. They're going to want to discuss you amongst themselves later."

Her expression soured playfully, and she threw a glare at Josie. "You're using me."

Josie nodded repeatedly. "Blatantly. You game?"

Rachel only hesitated a beat. "Yep. So long as we can swipe appetizers while we're up there."

Josie eyed Rachel almost proudly, then looked at David with a grin. "I like her, Grizz."

"That's what I was going for," he assured his cousin. "When I started seeing her, my only thought was, 'Will Josie like her?'"

Clint, their cousin Kate, and their brother Mike all snickered, which Josie ignored as she and Rachel swept upstairs, leaving the rest in the basement, still lounging on the furniture down there.

"Nicely done, Grizz," Kate murmured when the room was safe.

David glanced over at her. "Say what?"

She flicked her eyes meaningfully to the stairs, then back at him. "Your girlfriend. We've known her for all of two hours, and I'm ready for the wedding."

"Whoa, whoa," Mike protested with wide eyes, sitting up

straighter. "I'm slightly sleep-deprived from my seven-week-old, but did I miss something?"

"No," David insisted loudly. "We've only been together a few weeks."

Kate laughed in a dark, knowing manner. "Uh-huh. Sorry, Grizz, but you two are the real deal, and I think you know that."

He swallowed at the suggestion.

He *did* know that. He'd known that from the start. What he felt for Rachel was way more serious than anything he had ever felt for another woman in his life. Being with her was easy and exciting and exhilarating, and beyond all of that, it was fun. He was enjoying every minute of it whether they were in sweats or uniform or finery.

He just loved being with Rachel.

The idea of coming to Chicago to see Clint and the rest this weekend without bringing Rachel had never occurred to him.

That seemed significant, but he wasn't sure why.

"She's definitely the most attractive girlfriend you've ever had," Clint offered casually, tossing a balled-up, empty bag of chips at him.

David batted it away, hitting it at Mike instead, who caught it easily. "Now *that* is something I'll absolutely agree to. Way above my league."

"Says Mr. Number Eight in the hottie issue of *Sports Monthly*," Kate chortled.

The brothers roared in encouragement, grinning at David even as he glowered at his cousin. "You had to bring that up, didn't you, Kate?"

She shrugged, grinning her perfect orthodontist smile at him. "Did you think you weren't going to get eternal crap from us for this? I have at least five friends begging me for your number. Makes me regret that I have your poster up at work."

Clint raised his hand. "Give them my number, Kate. I'll console them."

"Helpful," she replied with a nod. "Really. So helpful."

"That's me," Clint quipped. "I dedicate my life to serving in any way I can. Not like my attention-seeking, pro-athlete brother. Such a selfish guy."

David looked at Mike in confusion. "Remind me why we let him live past six."

Mike shrugged a shoulder. "Mom liked him, and he made an easy fall guy."

"I knew it!" Clint shook his head in disappointment. "That explains so much."

David's phone rang, and he pulled it from his pocket, frowning at the name popping up on the screen. He rose and moved to one of the half windows across the room as he answered. "Hello?"

"Hey Grizzy, how's Florida?" Marcus's voice blared in his ear almost painfully.

"Dude, are you in your car?" he asked him, pulling the phone a little away. "Bellowing a little."

"Oh, sorry, man," his agent replied, his voice returning to a usual volume. "Right, you're in Chicago this weekend, right?"

"Right . . ." David said slowly, crossing one arm across his chest. "I told you that. Clint just got home."

"Right, right, tell him hi," Marcus said. "Great guy, that kid. Tell him to get back on the ice and I'll represent him too."

David rolled his eyes, and looked at Clint. "Marcus says hi, tells you to get back on the ice and he'll pick you up."

Clint held a thumbs up. "Meeting up with the old gang tomorrow, man. I'll send him pics of me in action."

"You hear that?" David asked Marcus, wondering where in the world this was going.

"Sure did!" Marcus actually sounded delighted, which was strange. Clint had been a fantastic hockey player, but his injury in college had kept him from the draft, and he'd never really talked about going back.

What did Marcus know?

"Right," Marcus said again, breaking in. "Good, good."

"Marcus," David broke in shortly. "I'm kind of with my family, and you're saying *right* so often I'm concerned things aren't right. What's up?"

There was a brief silence on the other end. "Unofficially and entirely hypothetically speaking," his agent eventually said in a casual tone, "would you be able to head up to Savery Field for a Flames game on Sunday and potentially sneak away for a very unofficial and nonbinding meeting with Jerry Berkley and Geoff Hammond?"

David blinked and barely avoided falling over sideways. He gripped the window ledge just in case the ground actually fell away. "They . . . They're asking?"

"They are," Marcus confirmed. "Been blowing up my phone for two weeks now. I'm finally feeling comfortable with potential terms, if Pittsburgh will play ball, but nothing has been decided, and it won't be for a bit. You know nothing could even possibly happen until mid-season, but they want to meet with you before talks get too far. And before you ask, no, you will not get in trouble for talking with them. I checked."

It was incredible. Impossible. Unfathomable.

The Flames had been *his* team growing up. He'd watched every game, had a dozen of their red shirts, collected all of the Ladder 521 cards they had released when the team had become sponsor of the Chicago Fire Department. They'd formed their own unofficial ladder company based at the stadium, hence the 521 number, the address of Savery Field itself.

And now the owner and general manager had asked to meet with him.

Were talking about him.

Wanted him.

"Okay," he said weakly. "I can do that."

"Thought you'd say that," came the laughing reply. "Get the whole family to go, and text me the number of tickets. They'll get you all on the list. Sound good?"

"Yeah." David swallowed with difficulty, then chewed the inside of his cheek for a moment. "Marcus, what if . . .?"

"They're not going to offer anything, man, and they're not going to trap you. You're not agreeing to anything, and they're not expecting you to. It's just a sit-down, face to face. Relax, okay?"

Right. Relax. When the offer of a lifetime could be on the table and he could have his actual childhood dream come to life in a matter of weeks.

Relax. Sure thing.

David hung up and stared at the phone for a second.

"Everything okay?" Mike asked in his best older-brother tone.

David turned to the rest of them. "Yep. I just got all of us tickets to a Flames game on Sunday, if we want."

"Oh, heck yeah!" Josie cheered as she, Rachel, his sister-in-law Keri, and his brother Tony came down the stairs. "Totally in!"

He nodded and smiled at Rachel, praying he would be able to hide this from her until it was actually something. The idea of leaving Pittsburgh right now, leaving her, right when they'd found each other, was like being lanced in the side.

He couldn't think about that. Not now.

"All right, ready for this?" Tony asked the group, rubbing his hands together. "Family karaoke is my arena."

Rachel looked at him doubtfully. "I find that hard to believe."

Clint howled with laughter. "Grizzy, bro, I want to kiss your girlfriend so much right now."

"I'll do it for you," David insisted, shoving his brother's face away as he passed him, and took Rachel in his arms, kissing her at once and dipping her dramatically.

A few whistles lit the room, while others told him to knock it off.

Rachel giggled and slapped his chest halfheartedly. "Dork," she muttered, her cheeks flaming. She looked at Mike with a smile. "Stacey's feeding the baby, so she says you have to defend your title alone, whatever that means."

Mike heaved a sigh. "Okay. Though Eighties Love Songs Champion is tough to defend as a solo."

Rachel gave them all a bewildered look. "Say what?"

The room laughed, and David pointed to the projector screen Josie had just switched on. "McCarthy Family Karaoke is a bit like Jeopardy. Categories are there."

He looked at the screen with her, laughing at the categories. Eighties Love Songs, Disney, Dad's Road Trip Faves, Songs We Hate, Crooning, and TV Theme Songs.

A slow grin crossed Rachel's face. "Oh, this is epic. And it is so on."

David slipped his arm around her waist and pulled her close.

She immediately looked up at him. "Hey, you okay?" she murmured as the others joked while they prepared.

He swallowed, then nodded. "Think so. Can't talk about it yet. I'm just . . . I'm really glad you're here."

She kissed his cheek lightly. "Me too, babe. How about we go out tomorrow night, just you and me? Clint says he's meeting up with some friends, and your brothers are having date night."

"Yeah," David agreed at once, nodding again. "Yeah. Let me show you Chicago, Rach. I'd like that a lot."

Casual time with David was one of Rachel's favorite things in the world. It was so easy to be with him, so comfortable and natural. The intimidation and nerves she had felt at the beginning of all of this had mostly faded as she'd come to understand him better and had gotten used to his smiles, his kisses, and that glorious body he kept so carefully hidden. Their schedules were so crazy that casual time was pretty much all that they had, and they took advantage of it whenever they could.

But formal date nights with David . . . Those were something special.

Her nerves roared to life with excitement and anticipation every time, like she was getting ready to go onstage and perform a number she loved.

Getting ready tonight had been especially entertaining. She'd brought a few options, not knowing what exactly the schedule of their time in Chicago would allow, but having the opportunity to go out just with David and to see the city with him was beyond any of her expectations.

The family lived forty-five minutes away from the city itself, and David insisted that they make the trip in, despite their going to the Flames game the next day.

"A night out with you is worth it," he'd told her with a wink when he'd sent her upstairs to get ready.

There was a very specific horde of butterflies within her

that only turned frantic when he did things like that, and it had taken forever for them to calm down.

Driving into the city with him now, she could barely look at him. There was something charged between them, and she was only too aware of the exact distance between them. She'd seen how his gaze had drifted up and down the length of her before they'd left, and a black jumpsuit had never felt so sexy in her entire life. She'd even gone for a loose cap-sleeve one instead of the halter or spaghetti-strap version Meghan had voted for. But this one felt more her style, and the teasing dip of the V-neck was too fun to pass on.

At the moment, the gold belt around her waist seemed too constricting with her nerves, and she could feel the pulse in her wrist almost clanging against the matching bangles. Even her gold caged sandals felt too tight, and she knew for a fact that they were a perfect fit. And good for walking around, unless they were in for a real haul.

Lands, she was evaluating her outfit on this drive, the city fast approaching. She was a mental mess, despite having managed the perfect smoky eye with her makeup and having the assurance from Megs that she was "freaking en hot pointe" with her look.

FaceTime with her best friend during the preparation phase had been inevitable.

She needed the vote of confidence.

Warm fingers suddenly slid along her wrist and up her palm and laced between her own fingers. She barely restrained a gasp as her other hand, out of David's view, gripped the edge of the side pocket of her door as her heart shot into her throat.

David raised the back of her hand to his lips, and Rachel exhaled slowly in response. Her fingers brushed against his knuckles in return.

"You okay, Rach?" he murmured over the soft-rock station they'd settled on earlier but hadn't really listened to.

She nodded, then wet her perfectly glossed lips quickly, turning her head to smile at him. "Yeah. This just feels more like the terrifying first date we didn't actually have."

He laughed as his thumb rubbed against her skin. "Okay, so it's not just me. That makes me feel better."

"You're nervous too?" She laughed, dropping her head back against the headrest. "You'd never know. You're as cool as a cucumber."

"Nervous isn't really the right word." His brow furrowed as he considered it. "Excited. Eager. Terrified."

Rachel made a sad sound. "Terrified of what, babe? I mean, I'm on a hot date with Grizz McCarthy on his home turf, I get nerves."

He gave her a very serious look before returning his attention to the road. "I think you underestimate the effect you have on sentient men, Rachel Bennett. People will forget my name with one look at you. Add to that your intelligence, your grace, your insane dancing abilities, and the best sense of humor I've ever met?" He shook his head slowly. "I'm swinging for the fence, and it's like I've forgotten how to bat."

An intense desire to kiss the man senseless lit up in the pit of her stomach, and all she could do was grip his hand tightly and look out of her window, biting down on her lip hard.

This whole thing was madness. She'd been in a few relationships in her life, some of them serious, but nothing like this. She was almost always on the edge of bursting into flame, even if they were on the couch in sweats, eating donuts. And it was the strangest thing; it was more like her best friend in the world had turned into a gorgeous hunk of a man with the best heart on the planet than that said gorgeous hunk of a man had taken an interest in her.

She'd known David for years, but it wasn't as though they

had been especially close. He was probably Sawyer's closest friend in the Six Pack, so she'd seen him more, but that was it.

Until her mom's wedding, Rachel could say that she hadn't really given him more thought than the others.

Okay, maybe a little more, but only because a tiny part of her had kind of always had a crush on him, but who didn't have a crush on Grizz McCarthy after five minutes with him?

But now . . .

David released her hand as they turned down a street and began to weave their way into the city of Chicago itself. Soon enough, he pulled the car into a crowded parking lot across the street from a brick building with a sign the shape of a grand piano, with blue-scripted neon lights across it that read *Syncopate*.

"Is this . . . a jazz restaurant?" Rachel asked, turning to David with a grin.

He shrugged, returning her smile. "Might be. All I know is they have fantastic food and good music." He quirked his brows and got out of the car, coming around to get her door and offering her a hand.

She smiled at it and placed her hand in his. "Such a gentleman." She let him pull her to her feet, standing too close to him, smiling up and inhaling the heady mix of his cologne and natural smell. "Who says chivalry is dead?"

His eyes darkened at once, and he brushed his nose against hers. "I give up. Who?" he murmured before gently kissing her lips.

Rachel shivered and stepped back for her own safety and sanity. "No idea. I just know someone does."

David laughed and locked the car, letting her take his arm as they made their way across the street. "Clearly *they* need to get out more."

"Or just meet you," Rachel pointed out.

He only shrugged, smiling to himself.

She sighed, leaning her head against him for a moment. She was going to have to get Aubrey McCarthy a present for raising this one, but what do you get the woman who gave the world such a perfect man?

This was going to require some thought, but surely she deserved something for her efforts.

Syncopate was the epitome of cozy and cool, its interior a throwback to a bygone era. Old pictures, exposed brick, and the right amount of mood lighting to transport its patrons to the classic jazz clubs of the forties. That combined with the smell of pizza, barbecue, and the faintest aroma of beer from the bar made Rachel smile as the waitress led them to their reserved table. This was a totally classic place.

"I don't even care how the rest of this night goes," Rachel told David quietly. "This is amazing."

He chuckled and gave her a bemused look. "You're easily entertained."

She whacked his arm lightly. "I am not! You have to admit, this is cool!"

"I know it is," he assured her. "That's why I wanted to bring you here. It's totally your style."

They sat across from each other at the table, and Rachel got distracted looking over at the live band playing, the members all looking the part. A few couples were dancing to the light song, some of them quite well, and Rachel's feet tapped beneath the table in anticipation.

"And I think we're going to hold off on dinner for the time being," David said to the waitress, who had come to take their orders, raising his voice in a blatant attempt to get Rachel's attention. "I think the lady needs a dance before we eat."

Rachel grinned brightly at him. "Really? Can we?"

The waitress laughed and gave David a look as she tucked her notepad and pen in her apron pocket. "You are a very smart man, sir."

David reached across the table for Rachel's hand, winking at her. "I'm a very *lucky* man," he answered, keeping his eyes on Rachel.

The song ended as they rose, and the slow, tantalizing strains of another began. A woman came forward to the microphone, her ebony hair swept back in a perfect forties wave, her dress cutting close to her shape as she swayed to the beat.

David led Rachel out to the dance floor as the woman began to sing. Rachel's previously racing heart slowed into a deep, slow pounding as she looped one arm loosely around his neck as he took the other and held it close to his chest. They moved in time with the music, keeping their eyes on each other, and Rachel had to smile at him.

"You're not going to judge my dancing, are you?" he murmured as a crooked smile spread across his lips.

She shook her head slowly. "Not at all. I'm just happy you're dancing at all. I would only want to dance here, tonight, like this, with you." A lump formed in her throat, and her fingers almost anxiously slid under the folded collar of his shirt. "Just you, David."

His smile faded, and the hand at her waist slowly pulled her closer to him until they were practically flush with each other. "I feel the same way, babe. There's only you. Only us, right?"

Rachel nodded as her eyes began to burn. She pressed her fingers gently against his neck, and he came to her, kissing her lips slowly, softly, then touching his brow to hers. She inhaled shakily, reveling in this moment. They were on the brink of something, she could feel it, and the weight of it was a pleasant one. She shifted her face to rest alongside his, her mouth at his shoulder, her arm curling around his neck further.

He held her just as close, the lyrics of the song sinking into them, swirling around them. There were no words for this, for anything about this moment. It *was* just them, and she would be perfectly content to never escape it. She closed her eyes, letting David lead, moving them to the music, getting lost in it, in each other. He was no dancer, but this he could do, and it was perfect.

"Rachel," he breathed at her ear, his voice barely audible over the band. "I have to tell you something."

Normally those words would scare her, but not now. Not with him. She turned her head to kiss his neck very softly. "What?"

She felt something ripple through him, and she smiled in total feminine satisfaction at it. "I'm . . ." He swallowed once. "I'm ninety-seven point three percent positive that I'm in love with you."

Rachel's heart skipped three beats, and for a moment, she pressed her face into his shoulder, inhaling deeply. Then she pulled back just enough to meet his eyes, one hand going to his jaw as she smiled ruefully. "What's up with the other two point seven percent?"

David grinned so beautifully she felt it in the center of her chest. "It's disappearing."

She nodded once, sliding her hand back to his neck. "Well, Mr. McCarthy, I'm ninety-eight point six percent positive that I love you too."

His breathless laugh touched her more than she could have said. Then he gave her a suspicious look. "And your stubborn one point four percent?"

Rachel gave him the slyest smile she could as the music continued to drive this moment between them. "It needs some convincing. Got any ideas?"

"A few," he replied in the most swoony voice she'd ever heard just before his lips were on hers again.

Chapter 12

"Oh, come on, there is no way that Hammersmith homers again. You were here for the third inning, right, Grizz?"

"I'm telling you, Mike, he's got the pitcher's number."

"I'll bet you the next round of hot dogs he doesn't."

"Tony, Mike, leave Davey alone. I think he's got a fair idea."

"Mom," all four McCarthy brothers groaned in eerie unison.

"Boys, be nice to your mother," Ed McCarthy ordered with the absent-minded response clearly born of years of fatherhood.

Rachel shook her head, caught in the middle of this McCarthy family craziness. They were all here for the game. Even Stacey and Keri had come with the kids, though it was complete madness. Mike and Tony seemed to do a decent job of being both fathers and baseball fans, though it was clear their wives understood how rare it was for the brothers to all be together and were letting them have this time together as much as possible.

The kids were obsessed with their uncle Grizz, so the

fathers didn't have to do all that much. Currently, it was David that had a little one on his shoulders, though Emily was only two and really didn't care about baseball at all. Her four-year-old brother, Eric, on the other hand, was passionate and screamed with all of his little boy delight at every good throw, hit, or antic by any member of the Flames.

It had been one of the best days Rachel had ever had with a family that was not her own, and she didn't think that lightly. The McCarthys had turned the day into a full-scale adventure, starting with a big breakfast at the house that Ed and Aubrey had made together. It would end sometime after this game with everyone lazily sitting around the firepit in the backyard talking about everything and anything, she was told, and she couldn't wait.

Tomorrow she and David would go back to Pittsburgh and back to the reality of their lives. But they would be going back together. Crazy in love.

She smiled whimsically now, clapping as Hammersmith *did* manage to hit another home run, much to the disgruntlement of the older McCarthy brothers, who now had to find the hot-dog guy.

Who'd have thought? Rachel Bennett was in love with David McCarthy, and he, amazingly enough, was in love with her.

Part of her really wanted something to pop up on the jumbotron across the field. The more rational part of her knew better than that, and the more feminine part of her wanted to keep it her secret. She wanted to gush over it while lying in bed at night, giggling in an insane way that no one would hear. She wanted to doodle all over a notebook and practice signing his last name. She wanted to watch all of the romantic movies in the world and imagine herself as the lead.

And she wanted to do all of it while keeping a perfectly

composed face in front of the rest of the world, without anyone else knowing that she had lost her mind.

And her heart.

Something cold touched her shoulder, and for a moment, she thought Meghan had appeared with another pint of ice cream for her overheated senses.

This time it was little Emily handing her a frozen chocolate malt, wearing David's trademark aviators, which were upside down. "For you!" the little girl chirped. "Cold."

Rachel took it from her, smiling broadly. "Thank you, Em. It is cold, isn't it?" She looked at David with a smirk. "How did you know this is my ballpark go-to?"

He shrugged, a crooked smile on his face. "Lucky guess." He shifted his niece on his shoulders, and the edge of his tattoo peeked out from the sleeve of his T-shirt.

Rachel touched it with a finger. "You know, I've never asked. Where did this tattoo come from? It's just a paw, isn't it?"

"I beg your pardon," Clint protested hotly from the other side of David. "I'll have you know that is Bear's paw."

Rachel gave him a look. "I'm not an idiot, Clint. Of course it's a bear paw; his name is Grizz."

The McCarthy boys laughed in the same tone and manner. "Not a bear, sweetheart," David told her with a twinkle in his eye. "*The* Bear. Our dog. Who was named Bear."

"Wait, what?" She looked down the line of brothers. "A dog? Did I miss a dog at the house?"

"Nope. The old boy's been gone for a while now." Clint pulled out his phone, flipped through some pictures, and held it out to her.

The largest dog she had ever seen in her entire life was there, laying at a much younger Clint's feet, looking more like a buffalo. It had black fur, and lots of it, and its tongue lolled happily out of its mouth. "What kind of dog is that?" she asked with a laugh.

"Newfoundland," Aubrey said from beside her. "Biggest cuddler on the planet. Thought he was a lapdog, which made for some interesting times."

"I bet." Rachel smiled at the picture, then looked at the brothers. "I see why you called him Bear."

David gave her a rueful smile as he craned his neck to look at the picture himself. "We named him before he was big. Clint wasn't particularly good with identifying animals. We had a fish named Bird."

She gave him a disparaging look. "You did not."

"We did too," the McCarthy clan replied as one.

She rolled her eyes and glanced at Keri and Stacey. "How do you put up with this?"

"Practice," Keri replied with a bland smile.

"And ice-cream therapy," Stacey added, giving her a meaningful look.

Rachel pointed at her in solidarity.

David checked his watch, then patted his niece's legs. "Sorry, Ems. Uncle Grizz has to get for a few minutes. You want to go to Daddy or Uncle Clint? Or Grandma?"

"Gramma!" Emily squealed, reaching for Aubrey with clenching fingers.

"Yes, baby?" Aubrey cooed as she leaned over and scooped her granddaughter up. "Come see Gramma and Papa, huh?"

Clint punched Tony in the arm with some force. "Dude!"

"What?" Tony cried, batting the brim of Clint's hat down.

"Your daughter hates me!" Clint protested.

"It's the Grandma factor," Mike pointed out as he fastened his baby to him in the carrier. "It trumps all other ties."

Tony gestured to their brother for the obvious truth.

"And before the popularity contest gets worse," David interjected with a playful shrug, "I'm ducking out! Be back in a bit." He gave Rachel a quick kiss on the cheek, then scooted out of the row and jogged up the stairs of the stadium.

Rachel watched him go, her brow wrinkling. She twisted her lips and looked at Clint as the Jacksonville Gators came up to bat. "Where's he off to?"

Clint shrugged with a half roll of his eyes. "Who knows? Maybe he knows a guy, maybe he's got a call from Marcus."

"He already had a call, remember?" Mike offered up as he jostled a little to settle the baby. "Friday. That's how we got the tickets."

"Marcus is needy," Tony said with a wave of his hand. "Clint's right, it's probably just a call. Maybe he'll finally get out of Pittsburgh."

Keri slapped Tony hard across the chest, and he shut up immediately, taking a long drink of his soda.

"Nah," Clint sputtered loudly, clearly covering what could have been an awkward silence. "The Knights need Grizzy at their helm. He's their only star. Marcus probably has another stupid promo idea like *Sports Monthly*."

Rachel swallowed and forced a smile as the rest of them bantered about what ridiculous schemes David could be forced into for his self-promotion.

She had a feeling what was going on *did* have something to do with Marcus and definitely had something to do with getting out of Pittsburgh. What could possibly be so important as to take him away from time with his family while they were in Chicago?

Except, perhaps, for an offer *from* Chicago.

Her throat clenched, and it was all she could do to avoid grabbing at it. She slid her hands into her back pockets instead, forcing her gaze out on the field.

David deserved to be here. To play for a team that could fill the stadium, instill this sort of passion in its fan base, and be in a city he loved so much. He deserved to have his dream fulfilled, though she knew full well he was happy to just play baseball. He could play anywhere and be satisfied.

She wanted more for him.

Just satisfied wasn't enough.

"Don't worry, sweetie," Aubrey murmured beside her even as she played a silly game with Emily, now safely in her grandfather's arms.

Rachel glanced at her. "Pardon?"

Aubrey gave her a warm smile, her bright-blue eyes not at all dimmed by the shadow of her baseball cap. "I said, 'Don't worry.' Whatever it is, I'm sure Davey will tell you. He's not much for secrets. He's not the most open man, but he's not that private either."

"He doesn't need to tell me," Rachel insisted with a shake of her head, returning her focus to the field. "It's none of my business."

The laughter of the woman beside her brought her back around. Aubrey's smile was still there, and she patted Rachel gently on the back. "I think it is your business, Rachel. I know my son, and I've never seen him like I've seen him with you. You care for him deeply, don't you?"

A lump formed in Rachel's throat, and she nodded as she tried to force it down. "Very much. It's just . . . It's all happened so fast, Aubrey. I've never . . . But I want . . ."

"Cat got your tongue, Rachel?" Ed asked with a very fatherly sort of smile as he leaned into the conversation.

Aubrey halfheartedly shoved him away. "Ed! This is why I'm glad we didn't have girls!" She looked at Rachel with a despairing smile. "It would have been chaos."

Rachel couldn't help grinning at them both. "I don't mind it. My dad was the same way."

Ed nodded firmly, his smile crinkling his gray eyes. "That he was. We could tell dad jokes with the best of them, Charlie and me. And embarrass our children to perfection."

"That I remember," Rachel said with a fond laugh. "The dad-section dance at that Albany game is still a favorite memory."

"What a claim to fame," his wife replied dryly. She put her arm around Rachel then and pulled her close. "You don't have to worry about David, sweetheart. He's the one who will worry. All he'll want to do is take care of you, even at his own expense. You just keep him on his toes and remind him that you are a partner, not a responsibility."

That took Rachel by surprise, and she searched the older woman's eyes. "You think he sees me that way?"

"I think my son loves you, Rachel," Aubrey told her bluntly. She flashed a quick smile. "Which, by the way, I am beyond ecstatic about." She sobered just as quickly. "David's loyalty to those he loves is also one of his obstacles. He's not going to know what to do, and he is going to need you there when he realizes that."

Rachel bit her lip very softly. "You want me to get out of his way?" she ventured, trying not to sound hurt.

Aubrey's eyes widened. "No! Oh heavens, no." She pulled Rachel in tightly and rubbed her arm with one hand. "I want you *with* him. You are a strong woman. An incredible woman. CAnd a real one. So genuine and so good for him. I want you to be his sounding board, his guiding star. I want you to bring out his best self and give him a run for his money."

"She wants a wedding, is what she wants," Ed chimed in.

"Ed!" Aubrey shrieked, making Rachel laugh even as her face flamed at the idea.

It was a great idea, in her mind, but not for a while yet.

Someday, it would be an amazing idea.

"I won't completely deny it," Aubrey muttered as she turned back to Rachel, her smile shy. "Your mom and I have talked . . ."

"Oh boy." Rachel hissed an exhale that turned into another laugh.

"I just want you both to be happy," Aubrey insisted. She rubbed her hand on Rachel's arm again. "And I think you could be. Relationships are partnerships, and I think you two could have it made."

What a statement coming from the woman who had raised four very successful, very handsome, very good men! A woman whom Rachel could easily consider a second mother and who knew David better than anyone Rachel could think of, possibly including the Six Pack.

On impulse, Rachel hugged Aubrey tightly, feeling a surge of affection for her and something stronger now binding them. "Thank you, Aubrey. And thank you for David, too."

Aubrey laughed and pulled back with a wink. "He is a pretty good guy, isn't he?"

"I helped," Ed reminded them both, looking mildly outraged as he bounced Emily. "Come on."

Rachel rolled her eyes. "Thank you, Ed."

He bowed a little. "You're welcome."

"Nice catch!" Clint roared from Rachel's other side as the crowd burst into applause, bringing all of them back to the game.

Rachel clapped absently, smiling for reasons that had nothing to do with the game. She might not know exactly what David's meeting, or non-meeting, was about, but she did know that she was in this relationship. She was absolutely in it, fully committed. Whatever it was, whatever may or may not come, she was in. All in, no holding back.

David was worth the risks.

They were worth it.

Weren't they?

Chapter 13

DAVID WATCHED THE relieving pitcher from the Minnesota Ice get in a few warm-up pitches, trying to get a decent feel for his tendencies. Not every pitcher had tells, and some were talented enough to surprise even the most observant of analysts, but this reliever had a comfort zone, and he was sticking to it.

Perfect.

The game had been going well enough, and the Knights were up by three runs, but David couldn't admit to being particularly focused. His mind was still reeling with the meeting in Chicago only days before and with the implications that meeting could have for him in the very near future.

Nothing had been offered, officially, and he had not committed to anything, officially.

They had danced around hypotheticals without being blatant in anything, all three men being as cryptic as they could be while keeping to a genuine spirit. David, for one, felt more like he was tiptoeing on a frozen pond with ice cracking beneath his feet than discussing, or not discussing, his future with one of the few teams he would actually express a preference in playing for. Most of the time, it was enough to simply be playing professional baseball, and he didn't care where he did so. There were dozens of teams out there, each of them with quality players and decent coaches, not to mention a fan base that would cheer them on no matter what.

Baseball was something special all over the country, no matter which city a team belonged to.

But Chicago . . . Chicago was home, and the Flames were his team. Not that he would have blinked all that much if the Spades had come calling, but he would have to avoid speaking with at least half of his family members for the duration of his contract, if not longer. Team allegiances were a precious thing in a city with two teams, and those allegiances were passionate.

He had left the meeting with Mr. Berkley and Mr. Hammond more confused than he had started it, but he would freely admit that Savery Field had never looked more beautiful to him in all its historic richness.

That had to mean something, didn't it?

David shifted his weight as AD stepped into the batter's box to start them off in this inning, and he clapped with the rest of the Knights in encouragement without saying a word. He hadn't told anyone in his family the details of his meeting, and he hadn't told Rachel either. He had nothing to tell, and that was the truth. All he knew was that the Flames were talking with Marcus, but so were a number of teams.

He couldn't treat this as any special circumstance. He couldn't get his family's hopes up.

And he couldn't get Rachel's down.

His chest clenched tightly at the thought of leaving Pittsburgh permanently. Of leaving her. They'd only been together for a few weeks, but it felt as though he had spent a lifetime loving her. Being with her. Having the gift of being able to turn to her, hold her, kiss her . . .

A tingle began in his lips at the thought, and he cleared his throat, narrowing his eyes on the batting of his team.

He couldn't think of Rachel during the game. Not if he wanted to keep his sanity in check. After all, no matter how much it felt as though they had shared a lifetime, it wasn't nearly enough for him.

Not nearly enough.

David glanced over at third base, where his old friend Steal was currently playing. They'd had a chance to chat before the game started, and the first time Steal had come up to bat he'd made some smart comment to David about how he'd look in a tutu.

The Belltown Bet was something the media looked forward to every time one of the Six Pack played another. Their antics had gotten out of hand a time or two, but for the most part, it was reasonable.

If Steal was talking tutus, he must have been in a great mood.

He didn't seem to be in one now. Sherlock was on third now, and David could see his lips moving. Every word he said seemed to make Steal tense further, and David didn't like that.

Two or three of the other guys in the dugout were laughing, and David looked at them carefully. They were eying the same interaction on the field that David was, but without any of the same concerns.

"Hutch," David called softly, picking on their designated hitter, who was a quiet guy most of the time.

Hutch came over with a smile. "Sup?"

David nodded towards their snickering teammates. "What's going on?"

His friend and teammate winced. "They've got some stupid plan to provoke your boy Cox on third. Lima, Tiny, and Crocket were egging him on when he was on base, and

Sherlock and Cowboy decided to join in while *they* were on base."

"You've got to be joking." David covered his face with one hand, sighing heavily. Steal had the shortest temper of anyone in the Six Pack and possibly of anyone David knew. He barely needed incentive to throw a punch, and here his own teammates were intentionally playing with fire. "Why?"

"Something about the Belltown Bet, I don't know." Hutch shrugged with a roll of his eyes. "Don't know why they don't just mind their own business."

David nodded, grinding his teeth. "A very good question, Hutch. Thanks."

Hutch clapped him on the back, then moved to get ready for his own turn at bat.

David stared at the rest of his teammates, wondering if he needed to shut them down now or let them hang themselves by their own stupidity when it didn't end well.

The Ice pitcher caught the hit straight from Hutch's bat, then tossed it to Steal at third. Steal tagged out Cowboy, coming in from second, then threw the ball to second, where T-Money was charging.

Smooth and easy triple play, and an ugly at-bat for the Knights.

David shook his head and grabbed his gear, heading for home plate. Though he'd done it every inning already, he raked the dirt around home plate and especially behind it with his cleats. The dirt could get packed down, and it changed how the ball bounced if it came off of a bat wrong. But it couldn't be too loose either.

Mindless superstition and habit, all of it. But it was part of his routine, his comfort zone on the field.

Sixth inning now, and the rest of the game still to come, but if he could have ended this game now, he would have.

He put the rest of his gear on and looked at the mound. Sherlock was angry about something, and that was never good. He only became more unpredictable a pitcher and less inclined to listen to David's advice.

Sherlock looked at David, though it was really more of a glare, and nodded once.

Oh goodie. This was going to be fun.

The first two Ice batters came and went without incident, one striking out, the other making it to first easily.

Then Steal came to the plate, and David could feel all the coolness of the entire state of Minnesota and the bordering Canada coming off of him.

"Easy, Steal," David murmured as he shifted his weight at the plate. "Come on."

Steal's grip on his bat tightened audibly. "You better tell your boys to back off, Grizz. They're getting to me. I'm about to snap."

David bit his tongue to keep from swearing. "I'll handle it. Stay cool."

Steal's chin dipped in a bare nod, his batter's stance solidifying.

Sherlock's first pitch screeched by without a swing from Steal.

"Strike!" the umpire hoarsely hollered.

David threw the ball back to Sherlock, signaling for a pitch he knew Steal couldn't hit.

Sherlock never even acknowledged him.

Come on, David thought furiously, signaling again.

But Sherlock came set, preparing to pitch, and then it was thrown.

The ball hit Steal in his left upper shoulder as he turned away from the impact.

"Dammit!" David roared as Steal threw his bat down, charging out to the mound. "Steal!"

But it was too late. The benches of both teams cleared, and Steal landed a powerful punch into Sherlock's jaw. The infielders were no help, taking Sherlock's side and egging on the fight.

David had no such loyalty. He shoved through them and grabbed Steal around the waist, using all of his might in an attempt to haul him off of Sherlock. One of the Ice players grabbed at David's jersey, and he glared at the fool.

"Are you going to get him out of here?" he demanded of him. "Huh?"

Sensing, rightly so, that he should stay out of it, the player turned to fight with someone else.

Steal was in no mood to be hauled away, but David moved his arms up until he could lock his hands behind Steal's neck, restraining his arms, and forced his friend to turn away.

"Come on, man," David grunted as he led him through the mass of players. "Come on."

"Get off!" Steal demanded, thrashing himself out of his hold. He whirled and stared at David, his eyes wild.

David held up a hand and pressed it to Steal's chest. "Stay. That's enough. Come on, walk it off."

Steal inhaled and exhaled rapidly, wiped at his bleeding nose, and shook his head, storming towards his dugout.

The umpire stopped him and threw him out of the game with too much dramatics for David's taste. Steal immediately got into a shouting match with the umpire, which his coaches took over, getting him out of there before worse punishment could come of it.

David rubbed at his eyes and looked back to the mound, where the more sensible players were separating the hotheads. He had no desire to get back into that mess, so he turned and walked back to home plate, perfectly content to wait until they could play again.

"What a mess, Grizz," the umpire said with a groan, craning his neck.

"Sherlock did that on purpose, sir," David replied as he spat into the dirt.

The ump gave him a look. "And Cox charged him. He could have just taken the walk. I stand by the ejection."

David nodded once, knowing better than to fight it. He waited for the field to clear, then sank into position as the next Ice batter approached.

"Still have to babysit your Belltown boy, huh, Grizz?" the batter sneered. "You gonna ground him next for shaming the Lumberjack?"

David got to his feet in one smooth motion, towering over the batter by a good six inches and at least thirty pounds. He said nothing, and the umpire put his hands between them, though it wasn't necessary.

The batter stared up at David with wide eyes, no longer confident or sneering in any way.

David stared right back, his jaw tight.

"Back off, gentlemen," the umpire barked.

The batter took a step back, out of the box, and pretended to check his bat, his throat moving on a swallow.

David slowly moved back to his position behind the plate, where he silently finished the inning and silently returned to the dugout and his team.

"Whoo!" Tiny bounded over to David as he came to the dugout. "Grizzy, that was beautiful! What did he say, huh?"

"Grizzy, I haven't seen you that fired up in ages!" Cowboy laughed. "I thought you were going to pound him, and we'd get round two!"

Lima slapped his thigh, cackling madly. "Hey Grizz, remember when you knocked Gavin Locke's lights out?"

"No."

"Yeah, yeah, and a petition went around to get your suspension pardoned?" Tiny added brightly.

"Nope."

"Locke had a black eye for like two months," Crocket reminded the group.

"Did he?"

Groans filled the dugout. "Come on, Grizz!" Tiny protested. "It's still got a hundred thousand views on YouTube."

"Don't remember, don't care," David said flatly. "Now everybody shut up and finish the game."

Thankfully, they left him alone for the rest of the inning and the rest of the game, as well as during showering and treatment after the game.

David only felt he could sigh when he left the clubhouse, and even then he was surrounded by reporters and photographers ready to capture the Belltown Bet for the news.

"Grizz! Grizz!" they called, randomly adding to the noise he was already dealing with.

He ignored them and pushed through without even a smile.

"Grizz!" an intrepid reporter he recognized from the local paper called, waving his hand. "How are you going to make Levi Cox pay for that fight *and* for losing? The Belltown Bet take brawls into account?"

David stopped, unable to move past the guy without addressing that. He turned and glared, just as he had in the sixth inning.

Everyone around him went quiet.

"I think," David said softly, "that Levi has been through enough tonight. Don't you?"

Without waiting for a reply, he pushed through the rest of the reporters towards the players' parking lot and pulled out his phone to text Rachel. He needed her, needed to hold her, needed her warmth . . .

"Hey you."

He looked up in surprise and paused when he saw Rachel there, waiting for him, leaning against his truck with a gentle smile.

He swallowed once, then moved into her open arms and let her hold him.

Chapter 14

Rachel felt like an idiot.

She looked great, her early rising and meticulous post-morning yoga routine seeing to a careful creation of a minimal-makeup appearance. When paired with black workout leggings, a loose T-shirt, and a Belltown fleece she'd swiped from David's closet last week, she was fairly confident she looked just right for a lazy Sunday morning. David didn't seem to care what she wore or how she appeared most of the time, but the flash of interest in his eyes was worth trying for.

What she was *not* so confident in was sitting on the steps of his condo in this upscale part of Pittsburgh, waiting for him to come home.

His beloved truck, which she'd secretly named Delilah on account of the axe decal on the back window, was in its usual spot, but he wasn't answering phone calls or texts. She could only conclude that he was out for a run, so here she would wait.

Like a moron.

In theory, it would be a perfect scene out of a romcom. The girl sitting on the steps of her beloved's home with a treat for him, knowing he might need some encouragement and love, while wanting to get some loving affection in return. It was the sort of staged-to-be-casual scene she'd seen a dozen times.

But this wasn't the chic setting of New York City, and the morning shadows were cold. Drivers cruising by gave her bizarre looks, and the smell of exhaust, combined with the sound of those cruising cars, just made for a pathetic scene.

Five more minutes. That was all she was giving him. Another shiver raced up her spine, and she rubbed her arms with a shake of her head.

"You're an idiot, Rachel Grace," she muttered, tucking a bit of hair behind her ear.

Still, something in her gut told her to wait, pathetic and idiotic picture or not. Last night's game had been miserable for him, and he hadn't said a word after. He'd just held her, and she'd held him back. She didn't know if he needed her to hold him again this morning, but her heart told her to go, so here she was.

The faint sound of shoes slapping on pavement made her perk up, and she looked up and down the sidewalk in anticipation.

Crossing the street onto David's block was the man himself, jogging in black basketball shorts and a faded gray Belltown T-shirt that had been cut down to a muscle shirt. The shirt was dark in places from sweat, and the wires of his headphones bounced against him with every step. His eyes were straight ahead and unfocused, his face flushed and glinting in the morning light.

He hadn't seen her, probably wasn't even looking for her, and one look at him told her there was a lot on his mind.

Rachel smiled softly for no reason at all as she watched him come closer. It was just good to see him. It felt right.

David's eyes flicked up to his condo, landing on Rachel as they did so. His brows shot up, and a smile parted his mustache from his beard adorably.

She waved a little and awkwardly stood, shoving her hands into the pockets of the fleece jacket.

David stopped in front of her and pulled his earbuds out, yanking the iPod strapped to his arm off and shoving both into his pockets. "Good morning, gorgeous."

Rachel grinned. "Hey, hot stuff."

His warm laugh sent a wash of heat through her, and the way his eyes moved to take her in sent a blush into her face that she was sure matched his own coloring at the moment. "To what do I owe this gift?" he rumbled with interest, taking a step towards her.

She lifted her shoulder in a shrug. "I thought you could use a treat."

He surprised her by slipping his hands into the pockets of her jacket and tugging her down a step, bringing her almost flush with him. "I sure could," he murmured just before his lips descended on hers.

Within the pockets of the jacket, she laced her fingers with his and clung tight. Arching up on her toes, she leaned into the kiss as much as she was able, keeping her lips soft, letting him take the lead however he wanted to. There was an edge of need in his kiss that made her heart ache, though she didn't understand why.

David broke off before she expected and kissed her brow very softly. "Seeing you here waiting for me, wearing my jacket, I might add, is the best treat I could ever ask for, babe. I can't even tell you how much it means to me."

Rachel smiled, tilting her face up to kiss him on the lips. "The jacket smells like you. I've been wearing it nonstop since I swiped it."

He laughed again, his fingers toying with hers as they still lay contained in the pockets. "Do you know what that sort of thing means to a guy, Rach? We get all kinds of primal, possessive feelings."

"Oh good," she replied, quirking her brows. "I was hoping it was like that."

Now he threw back his head and laughed, sliding his hands out from the pockets and setting them at her hips. "You were, huh? I love you so much." He shook his head and kissed her quickly. "Come on in. I need a shower before I hug you good and proper."

Rachel turned and grabbed the bag she'd had sitting beside her the whole time. "I also brought donuts."

David paused on the step, still smiling at her. "Woman, you are perfection."

"I do try," she demurred with a little curtsey.

He shook his head and let them into the condo, kicking off his shoes in the entryway before taking her hand and leading her back to the living room. "You okay to hang out here for five minutes? Forage all you want in the kitchen, TV remote is there. Don't DVR any of your home-renovation shows while I'm gone."

Rachel put her hands on her hips as she faced his grin. "Excuse you. You can't give me control of the remote and then dictate what I do with it."

"Can too." He raised a daring brow. "My house, my rules."

Narrowing her eyes, Rachel slowly moved towards him, a surge of satisfaction roaring to life as his grin, and his smugness, faded with every step. "Oh really?" she drawled on her way to him.

His throat constricted with a swallow, his blue eyes fixed on her.

She stood nearly toe to toe with him, then brought a

finger to the paw tattoo on his arm. She slowly traced the edges of it, just as she'd imagined doing at least a dozen times since she'd seen him in *Sports Monthly.* Her lips curved as goose bumps began to rise on his skin.

"Well," she murmured as she continued to trace it. "My man, my rules. Right?"

Some incoherent noise emitted from him but seemed trapped somewhere in his chest and throat, making her smile spread. She took one step around him and pressed her lips to the center of his tattoo. "I'm going to take that as a yes, David," she told him, her lips still in contact with his skin. "That okay?"

He only exhaled, making her giggle and kiss his arm lightly before stepping away and moving back to the couch. "Have a nice shower."

She didn't hear him move, so she glanced back at him.

David was still standing there, staring at her, his eyes impossibly blue. "You don't play fair, Rachel Bennett," he growled. "And I'm this close to forgetting the shower and shamelessly taking advantage of you right there on my couch."

Rachel choked out an almost-hysterical laugh. "No! Go shower, you dork! I'll sit right here, prim and proper, and if you're quick, I won't even start eating donuts without you."

"I never thought I'd say this, but donuts aren't even on my mind right now. Or on my breakfast menu."

Her eyes shot to his, her laughter freezing in her chest as her body stilled. He was completely and entirely focused on her, and she wasn't sure she'd ever realized just how powerful he looked. How completely masculine and hopelessly addicting. Raw and beautiful, and, somehow, he was hers.

Something hot began to curl in the pit of her stomach, reminding her of that overheated feeling she'd had seeing the magazine, but this was so much more.

This was all-out combustion of everything she thought, knew, or had ever felt.

Rachel inhaled a very unsteady breath, then exhaled it very slowly. "Whoa," she whispered, the tension between them robbing her of anything coherent or intelligent to say.

"Yeah." He swallowed and cleared his throat. "Yeah." He ran a hand through his hair, then turned and strode out of sight, moving up the stairs to his bedroom.

Freed from that mind-blowing moment, Rachel slid down the leather couch and covered her face with her hands, focusing on inhaling and exhaling.

Was it possible to actually die from wanting a man so much? Or from loving him so hard she felt sick at the moment? This was the most ridiculous thing she had ever felt, and the continual waves of intensity overwhelmed her.

She was playing with fire, and she had been burned. The best kind of burned, a fun and, quite frankly, really hot kind of burned, but not something she should play with anymore.

Or, at least, not very often.

Not if she wanted sanity or to not end up trying to explain to her brother about her relationship with David as Sawyer walked her down the aisle of their shotgun wedding.

Even the mental picture made her giggle, and she dropped her hands, staring up at the ceiling as she lay on the couch in a puddle of melted goodness.

Sawyer. She had to tell him at some point. She'd avoided posting any pictures of her and David, more for protecting his privacy than anything else, but it wasn't fair for their relationship to be getting so serious and so deep without Sawyer knowing.

Her mom had promised not to say anything, but Rachel knew it was killing her not to gush about them to her friends. The moment she did, all of Belltown would be in on the gossip, and they'd never be able to go back without someone saying something about it.

And when Belltown knew, so would the world.

The Six Pack had that sort of effect and that kind of pull.

If she played with fire and melted into couches on David's account much longer, the news would break somewhere else before Sawyer knew.

He deserved better than that.

Rachel sat up and pulled out her phone, looking up the Knights' schedule quickly.

"Tweeting pictures of my bachelor pad?"

She looked up to see David there in jeans, pulling a shirt over his head, his washboard abs on blatant display for just long enough to make her mouth go completely dry.

Rachel blinked as a hard rush of air came out in an exhale she didn't know she had in her. "Syrup," she muttered.

"What?" David asked with a laugh, a hand rubbing hard through his hair and sending water droplets flying.

Face flaming, Rachel shook her head. "Nothing. Come here, I have a question."

He sat beside her and dropped an arm around her, pulling her against him, his attention on her phone. "What's up?"

She nestled into him and showed him the screen. "You're in Columbus next weekend. What if I drove over for the Saturday and Sunday games? And . . . we told Sawyer about this?"

David frowned very slightly in thought, then nodded. He looked at her with a smile. "Okay. It's about time, wouldn't you say?"

Rachel lowered her eyes to his chest. "Probably past it, honestly."

He pressed two fingers to the underside of her chin and brought her eyes back to his. "Hey."

She blinked and swallowed. "What?"

He stroked her chin as though it were porcelain. "I love you. It'll be okay."

"I love you too," she whispered, leaning in for a kiss, then lying against him and letting him hold her tight.

She felt David press a kiss against her hair, and she wrapped her arms around his chest, sighing heavily and closing her eyes.

He shifted for a moment, something rustling, then poked her gently in the shoulder. "Donut?"

She nodded once and opened her mouth, snickering in surprise when he stuck the whole thing between her teeth.

Saying he would do something and actually doing the something were two very different matters.

Skeeter hadn't pitched the game last night, so they'd had a chance to chat before the game. He asked how Steal had been after the ejection last week, and David asked how beating Axe Man's team so badly had felt. They'd laughed a little, and that was about it.

Nothing about Rachel was mentioned. Nothing about Chicago was mentioned.

They hadn't gone out after the game, as Skeeter had serious habits surrounding the night before a game. Eating out would come tonight. If Skeeter wanted anything to do with him ever again.

Despite his assurance to Rachel that everything would be fine, David wasn't so sure. The more he thought about it, the worse the possibilities became.

He'd been on pins and needles the entire course of the game, and none of his teammates had been able to pull him out of the funk. David wasn't sure he'd entirely forgiven them for the debacle that had been the Ice game, but he wasn't giving anyone the cold shoulder either. He couldn't afford to let personal things like that get in the way of working as a team and playing the best game of baseball possible.

Skeeter wasn't as easily razzed as Steal, so none of the Knights bothered with it, which was much appreciated from David's perspective.

None of them knew that he was going to confess to one of his best friends that he was dating, and was in love with, his sister. Provocation from David's team, under the circumstances, might have put a damper on that.

The game had ended with a last-minute home run from Mace, the popular Black Racer catcher, which had brought the Black Racers the last few runs they needed to win the game. As that brought the weekend's games between them to one win apiece, no one was expecting the Belltown Bet to come to anything until the final game tomorrow.

Unless they were counting that Skeeter had struck David out in the fourth inning.

Either way, he was paying out tonight, though not in a way the media would have liked to record for its news cycles.

Nothing silly or over the top, and nothing too embarrassing either. Just something that could significantly impact one of his best friendships and would bring him to a point of vulnerability that left him on the edge of a panic attack to even consider.

Rachel would be with him, he reminded himself. She was in this too, and Skeeter wouldn't find it easy to move her from the current position. They were a team, and this was what they wanted.

Surely Skeeter would want Rachel's happiness above all else . . .

What if he didn't think David could manage that?

David swallowed with some difficulty as he left the

visiting-team clubhouse at the Black Racers' park, forcing a smile and a wave for the media lingering around.

"Grizz! Grizz! Have you and Skeeter settled on the terms of the Belltown Bet yet?" someone called out.

David paused briefly, still smiling. "We're working on it. We'll find out tomorrow, won't we?"

The reporters laughed, then turned to talk to some of the stars from tonight's game.

David had taken great care to not be one of them. Oh, he'd played a great game, but nothing especially noteworthy or spectacular. He just did his job and coached from the field as best as he could. Nothing major, but he'd called the pitches and called an infield meeting when he'd noticed a tendency from a few of the guys to lead off more than usual. Coach Barker had given him a solid high five for that one, considering they'd nailed a sweet double play right after.

It was his unofficial position, his pseudo coaching, and he took it seriously. Coach Barker was perfectly content to let David call it as he saw it, especially since he was right more often than not. Some of his teammates didn't seem to like it or respect his acting in it, but he wasn't about to give that up.

Cooler heads didn't always prevail, but at least they could see a bit more clearly.

In theory, anyway.

At the moment, he wasn't seeing much at all in his anxiety-fueled tunnel vision.

He moved out to the parking lot, where Rachel had told him to go, praying she had already touched base with her brother and put him in a good mood. Skeeter had played a great game too, pitching one of his best games so far this season, which ought to bode well.

But would anything prepare him for this?

After walking for what felt like half an hour, he found the

siblings leaning against Skeeter's beloved Mustang, Ellie. Skeeter had an arm draped around his sister's shoulder, and the two of them were laughing uproariously.

David managed to smile at that. "You park far enough away, dude? You'd think the pitcher would get premier parking here."

Skeeter rolled his eyes and looked at Rachel. "You hear the bitterness in his tone? He's still whining about pitchers and catchers."

"Hey, I got lost out here," Rachel pointed out, jabbing her brother in the side with a finger. "Thought you were going to have an ambush waiting for me or for him." She looked up at the lights of the lot, looking speculative. "I'm shocked the lights even work this far from the stadium."

"Ha ha," her brother remarked dryly. "You're both very funny. I don't like premier parking; it puts Ellie at risk."

"Ooh," David and Rachel said as one in the same tone, drawing out matching smiles.

"Knock it off," Skeeter ordered with a scowl. "You'd feel the same way if you put as much work into her as I have."

David nodded with as much false understanding as he could. "I'm sure I would."

Skeeter heaved a dramatic sigh and pushed off of his car. "Well, should we go? I know the Knights are picky about curfew for their MVPs."

This time, David couldn't laugh at the jab. He needed to get this out now, or he wouldn't manage it at all. A parking lot outside of a baseball stadium wasn't a great scene for the discussion, but options were limited.

"Actually, Sawyer," David said with a faint clearing of his throat, using his friend's real name instead of his usual nickname, "I need a word."

Skeeter's eyes went round, and he glanced at his sister,

who stared at David without blinking. "Okay," Skeeter said slowly, returning his attention to David. "Go on."

David flicked his eyes to Rachel, whose chin dipped in a nod, giving him the last bit of courage he didn't know he'd needed. "It might be a little late to tell you now, but . . . Rachel and I have been seeing each other. Dating. Seriously, in fact. As serious as it gets."

His friend's brows rose, but he said nothing.

Not sure if that was encouraging, David kept going. "I can't put a moment on when I started to see Rachel as more than just your sister, but there was your mom's wedding, and then we bumped into each other in Pittsburgh a couple of times, and then the Hall of Fame thing in Belltown . . ." He paused for a swallow, his throat tightening almost painfully. "And we've talked every day since then, that I can say for sure. And it's not enough. I mean, it is enough, but I want more. I mean . . ."

He ran a hand through his hair, cursing himself. This was going nowhere, and it was spiraling fast. There was only one thing he could say to possibly salvage his confession.

"I love Rachel," he admitted, his voice rising just a bit more than it should have with its bluntness. He looked at her and felt the tension within him slowly ebbing away at her smile. "I'm absolutely crazy about her. And the more time I spend with her, the crazier I get. She's the most incredible woman I've ever met, and she's become my best friend. I want to give her all the stars in the sky and anything else she's ever wanted in her entire life. And yes, I know what a sap that makes me sound like."

Rachel's smile widened, and he could see love beyond words shining from her eyes.

He exhaled softly with relief, then returned his focus to Skeeter, who did not have love of any kind shining from anywhere within him. "I know I'm breaking unwritten Six Pack rules, not that we ever thought we needed to make this a rule, and the bro code, and the former teammates pact, and whatever else feeling this way is a violation of. I'm willing to break them all because your sister is worth it. Rachel is worth absolutely everything."

His voice failed him for a moment, and he fought to get it back, straightening. "So if you want to use me as a punching bag or run me over with Ellie, go ahead. I'm not giving Rachel up. Take your best shot."

Skeeter stared at him, his expression unreadable, though it was clear from the subtle motions of his jaw that he was grinding his teeth.

Oh boy.

"You're right," Skeeter finally said, his tone as tight as his face. "He went for dramatic."

David frowned, completely lost.

"He means it though," Rachel replied, keeping her eyes on David. "That's what I'm saying."

Skeeter looked at his sister in bewilderment. "Well, do you think I'd let you be with a guy who wasn't genuine? Please. Also pay up." He held out a hand.

David watched in shock as his girlfriend pulled a twenty-dollar bill from the back pocket of her jeans and slapped it into her brother's hand. "What is this?" he demanded.

Rachel giggled and covered her face with one hand. "I'm so sorry, babe. I told Sawyer you would go for dramatic, and he said you'd tell him before we ever left the ballpark."

He looked between the siblings, his emotions going off in nine different directions. "You told him?"

Skeeter chuckled and shook his head. "Easy, Grizz. I guessed. Interrogated Rach on the phone the other day and made her swear not to tell you that I knew. Had a great conversation with my mother last night about the whole thing."

Rachel shoved her brother so hard he stumbled. "You did not! Oh, Sawyer . . . Mom is going to be beside herself." She threw her hands in the air. "I'm going to have to call her tonight when I get back to Erica's. So much for our all-nighter."

Skeeter looked at his sister as though she had lost her mind. "It's already ten thirty—why are you two staying up all night?"

"You don't get to interrogate me about my relationship without getting the same, dear brother," came the beautifully snarky reply. "Only I don't play as nice. Erica promised to dish and supply ice cream, which is why she's letting us all have this little rendezvous without her. Now, let's go, I need french fries." She gestured to the car, and Skeeter groaned, marching over to get in.

David hadn't moved a muscle, and he could only stare at Rachel.

She looked back at him, the amusement in her face fading. "Oh, honey . . ." She came over to him and took his hands. "You okay? You're not upset, are you? It was a great game tonight, and you were awesome. You'd have had them if Kyle had thrown Mace a curve like he gave Sawyer."

"He knows," David said, shaking his head in disbelief. "And he hasn't run me down."

Rachel gaped for a second, then broke into a grin. "I know. Well, he would never run you down with Ellie, he'd rent something for that."

David felt a hoarse laugh escape at that. "True." He looked through the windshield at Skeeter, who was watching the two of them in blatant amusement. "He's . . . he's okay with this."

"He is. Isn't that amazing?" Rachel slipped her arms around his waist, and he reciprocated. "He thinks it's a great idea, and he claims he's known forever."

They both rolled their eyes. "Right," David said with a snort. He exhaled and touched his brow to hers, relief making him slightly woozy. "How could he have known forever when we didn't?"

"Exactly." Rachel arched up and kissed him hard, then followed it with a gentle encore. "I love you, you know. And it was almost impossible to keep from jumping you when you were confessing your feelings in front of my brother and practically daring him to run you down for my honor. It was very attractive."

"Was it now?" David pulled back a little, giving her a speculative look. "How attractive?"

Rachel went to her toes again, brushing her nose against his. "Very," she repeated in slow, emphatic tones that made him instantly break out in a sweat.

A horn honked just behind them, making both jump.

"Let's go, lovebirds!" Skeeter demanded. "I'm hungry, and my girlfriend is waiting. Get in or walk!"

David groaned and kissed Rachel quickly. "Well, at least we don't have to hide this anymore."

Rachel linked her fingers through his as they walked around to the car doors. "No, we don't, do we?"

CHAPTER 15

"I DON'T KNOW why you're so nervous. You're the only possible choice for the lead."

"The roomful of dancers who auditioned would contradict that statement."

Rachel's forearm was suddenly slapped and slapped hard. "Ow!" she protested with a glare at her friend.

Meghan was unperturbed. "Knock it off. You know as well as I do that you could outjump any of these wannabes on one leg and spin circles around them at the same time."

"That sounds painful." Rachel looked around the room, her stomach clenching and unclenching in a nauseating way. She'd been working her butt off to nail the audition piece for their next show. She hadn't been lead in anything in ages, and while Andante certainly gave her opportunity enough to perform, most of it wasn't anything she could seriously consider part of her portfolio. Nothing she could really sink her teeth into.

She hadn't been able to make anything of herself in New York, and she had yet to make anything of herself in Pittsburgh. She'd spent many random nights on her couch avoiding the world while shoving her face with junk food to fend off real despair over that.

"I got an email from Annette Harper," Rachel murmured before her chest could begin to constrict spasmodically with panic. "She's offered me a teaching position at her academy in Baltimore."

Meghan whistled softly and nudged her. "You thinking about it?"

Rachel nodded. "If I don't get this, I'm seriously thinking about it."

"You *will*," Meghan assured her. "You're long past your big break. Grizz will be beside himself when he hears."

That made Rachel smile, though it was very tight. She hadn't told David about this. He was under too much stress and strain as it was, and he wasn't sharing his reasons. This wasn't her version of doing the same thing; she just didn't think he needed more to worry about.

And he would worry. He was always worrying about her for something or other. The other day it was if Sawyer was teasing her too much about them, then it was if she was really okay with him traveling so much, and then it was if she minded him telling other people about their relationship. It was adorable, and it was maddening.

If she didn't love the guy so much, she might have punched him in the gut for driving her crazy. As it was, she would have broken her hand on his abs, and she couldn't afford the injury.

She was in the process of making a Team Grizz T-shirt to wear to his next home game just to let him know how she felt about others knowing about their relationship.

The Six Pack alone would blow up both of their phones over it, and it would be glorious.

Right now, she would take the ribbing from her adoptive brothers over sitting here in this agony.

Monica and Doug came out onto the stage then, and the entire room fell silent too quickly. Evidently, everyone was just as anxious for answers as she was. Which meant everyone in the room also had hopes that they had done enough for the part. And probably had.

Yay.

"I feel sick," Rachel muttered, sinking lower into her seat.

Meghan clicked her tongue and shook her head. "Come on, this isn't any worse than the other shows recently."

"Yes, it is," she replied in a whisper. "This is a specific lead for a jumper. That's me. This is it, Megs. If I didn't nail this . . ."

"Don't give yourself ultimatums," her best friend snapped. "You're giving me heartburn."

Rachel clamped her lips together, her teeth clenching so hard her jaw already ached.

"Good morning, Andante," Monica said into the microphone while Doug simply struck a ridiculous pose next to her. "Thank you to everyone who came in for the last round of auditions this morning and to the rest of you who took advantage of free-range rehearsal. I know you've all been anxious about the announcing of the leads for our next show, and we've been working hard on picking the right dancers for each role."

Doug nodded at every word, pursing his lips together like he was preparing for a selfie on Instagram. "That's right," he added, though he took no trouble to lean closer to the microphone and be clearly heard.

Whatever.

Monica slid her glasses down from on top of her head and lifted the clipboard she carried. "Alrighty, let's get this going. First, the interpretive lead for female, Angela Price. Male interpretive lead, Colby Rogers."

The room applauded their support, and Rachel's heart began to pound frantically.

"Main lead for female," Monica went on, "and this one was really tough. But we are excited to announce that, for the first time, Missy Cross will be our star!"

Applause and cheers filled the room, and Rachel felt her lungs simply disappear within her. She stared at Monica and Doug in outright betrayal, her jaw slowly falling further and further as she stared.

Monica's eyes darted to her quickly, and Rachel saw her swallow before returning her attention to the clipboard. Doug looked at her too, but he was only superior in his regard.

They went on to mention Missy's partner for the show, but Rachel suddenly couldn't hear anything other than Meghan's stream of swearing beside her.

Rachel wanted to get up from her seat and storm out of the auditorium like a diva. She wanted to feel joy that someone who worked as hard as Missy was getting her shot. She wanted to call her mom and burst into tears, blubbering incoherently while her mother murmured, "Oh, sweetie," over and over again.

But at the moment she could do none of those things. She had to sit here like a good company member and wait for the entire cast of auditioned parts to be announced.

She had put all of her eggs in one basket this time, and someone had scrambled the damn things.

Company billing again, probably without even an opportunity for a solo or duet piece.

Meghan would get one; she was the best ballet-style dancer in the group, so auditioning wasn't even something she had to do, though she did it anyway. And maybe Monica would give Rachel a pity piece as an apology. Colby would try and pull some strings. He was good to her like that.

But if she couldn't nail an audition in her specialty with a small company, what was she doing still dancing?

Why was she even here?

Meghan gripped her hand tightly, but Rachel couldn't squeeze back.

She waited until the announcements were over, then, when they were dismissed, she moved past Meghan without a word and headed for the back of the auditorium with everyone else. No one looked at her, and she didn't look at them. Meghan didn't call after her, thankfully, as that would have attracted way too much attention, and that was the last thing that Rachel needed right now.

Once outside, she turned away from the parking lot, where everyone else was going, and headed towards her apartment. It wasn't a far walk, and she needed the air.

Inhale, exhale. Inhale, exhale.

She ought to call Annette and ask for more details about the academy in Baltimore. That was the next logical step.

But Baltimore was too far away from David, and she suspected that he would be getting traded soon anyway. Who knew where that would take him? She needed to take advantage of every moment she could while they were in the same city.

If only he were here now.

The lump in her throat turned into a choked cry, and she pulled out her phone, wiping at a tear that was leaking from the corner of her eye.

She had placed the call before she knew it, and she held the phone up to her ear, lengthening her stride and the speed of each step to ward off her impending sobs.

She couldn't cry on the phone to him on a game day. It would drive him crazy, and he would call Cole and get home to her instead of playing in the game or something ridiculous like that.

It rang three times, and Rachel sighed, knowing the next step was voicemail.

"Hello, my love," a deep and sleep-drunk voice rumbled in her ear.

She smiled at hearing it, despite the stress running through her veins. "You have no idea how amazing it is to hear you like this."

"Half dead?" David growled, his voice faintly muffled. "Why is that amazing?"

Rachel hummed softly. "Your voice is all raspy and rough. You're making my toes curl in my shoes, and my palms are beginning to sweat. And when you say 'my love' . . . " She shuddered breathily for effect. "So good, babe. So, so good."

He cleared his throat, and she bit back a giggle. "Stop turning me on this early in the morning," he told her. "Hutch won't appreciate me screeching in a cold shower as his alarm."

Idiot. Rachel slapped her forehead with a hiss, her amusement fading immediately. "Crap. Time change. I am so sorry, babe, I completely forgot where you were."

"For you, my love," he rumbled pointedly, making her smile again, "there is nothing wrong with six o'clock." She heard him rustle and imagined him turning over to sit up in bed. "Now, if we hadn't played into extra innings last night and had gotten in before midnight, I might be slightly more coherent, but talking to you is never a disappointment."

Rachel swallowed a fresh lump and slowed her step, exhaling slowly. "I love you," she murmured with heartfelt tenderness. "So much."

"Good," he grunted. "This would be so uncomfortable one sided."

She laughed, then sighed. "Oh, babe. I needed to laugh. Thanks."

"You okay?" he said at once. "It's a bit early to be done with practice for you."

"Oh yeah." She waved her hand, though he wouldn't see the dismissive motion. "We only had light stuff today. Some people were auditioning for parts for the next show, so the rest of us just messed around."

He was silent for a moment. "You're not that great at lying, hon. What's up?"

"I'm fine," she assured him, forcing herself to sound more natural. "That really is what we did today. I just . . ." She inhaled quickly, wincing. "I miss you. I want to come over to your place and have you make me an omelet, then sit on your couch in sweats and fight over blankets. I want you to hold me and kiss me until I almost pass out. I want you to walk around shirtless so I can shamelessly check you out and . . ."

"I'll get Cole's jet," he suggested lightly. "That sounds amazing, particularly where I kiss you until you almost pass out, although I don't actually recommend passing out. I could give you a foot rub, and I'll do it shirtless just for you. I'd even try yoga again for you, though I'd probably spend the whole time making inappropriate comments about your extreme hotness."

Rachel groaned in delight, smiling against her will. "Yoga with Grizz, I can see the DVD collection now. It'll be the most epic workout series ever, and it'll always be out of stock."

"I'll be set for life. Wouldn't have to play baseball ever again."

"Yes, you would," Rachel told him with a laugh. "You love baseball too much to stay away."

David grunted. "You're probably right. And I'm pretty good at it, I guess."

"You're an all-star, babe. Kick Axel's trash tonight, okay? No more extra innings, no questions. Destroy him." Rachel grinned at nothing at all, imagining she was smiling at him. "And tell Hutch that Axel sucks at backpedaling to his left."

"How in the world do you know that?" David demanded with a laugh. "Shut up, Hutch, go back to snoring." He mumbled something Rachel didn't catch, then lowered his voice. "I love you, babe, but I'm not sure I've heard anything hotter than you talking about Axel's sweet spot. Or sore spot, as it were."

"Come back soon," Rachel purred, "and I'll tell you everything I know about Levi's tell for when he's about to steal."

David made a hissing sound that made her snort with laughter. "Deal. So hot, Rachel. So freaking hot." He cleared his throat again. "Hey, for real though, when I do get back, we need to talk. There's something we need to discuss."

Rachel stilled. "That sounds serious," she said slowly. "You're not breaking up with me, are you?"

"Hell no," he told her emphatically. "I'm in love with you, and that's not going away. No, we just need to talk, okay?"

"Okay." Rachel shook her head, exhaling. "Okay. Bring me ice cream if I'm going to cry."

"I love you," he replied, his voice turning low and rumbling again. "And I hope you don't cry."

"Love you, too. Still want that ice cream."

"Yes, ma'am."

Rachel smiled as she hung up, and pressed her tongue to the front of her teeth. There was only one thing he would need to have a serious talk with her about that wouldn't involve breaking her heart.

Someone had made an offer, and he was considering it.

CHAPTER 16

"Inhale, exhale. That's all, just inhale and exhale."

Easier said than done, even to himself.

It would be fine. Fine, really. Rachel would be okay, and no one would cry.

Okay, *he* might cry, but she wouldn't. She was stronger than he was.

She'd better not cry. He wasn't sure what that would do to him, and he was afraid of that unknown reaction.

Which was why he was on this errand before he faced her. He needed reinforcements just in case.

Ice cream, which was easy enough—she had very particular tastes—and flowers.

He swallowed hard. That was intimidating.

His phone was out and the call placed before he blinked twice.

"Hello there!"

"Mamma Sal," he gasped without preamble. "I need help."

"Okay, what's wrong?" Her tone was all maternal business, and he forced himself to calm down.

"Nothing, I promise," he assured her, smiling to brighten his tone. "I just need to get flowers for Rachel."

There was silence on the other end. "I think we've had this conversation, sweetie. After-the-show flowers, right?"

"No, no, I need specific flower advice."

"Honey, you have a mother. She's a woman, and—"

"I need to know Rachel's favorite flower," he interrupted, wincing as he wound his way through the grocery store and headed for the frozen-food section.

Again, there was silence. Then a heavy sigh. "Proposal or apology?"

David laughed once in surprise. "Neither. It's more of a preemptive strike. A just-in-case-I-need-them."

"That sounds serious," Mamma Sal laughed, making him relax. "Oh! Is this because she didn't get the part? She was pretty upset."

Hand on the pint of ice cream, he paused. "Wait, what? What part?"

"Uh-oh."

David's shoulders slumped, and he shook his head, pulling the pint out and closing the freezer door. "That's what the call was all about," he muttered. "She didn't say a word."

"Pretend I didn't, okay? Please, David. If she wanted you to know, she would have told you."

"Mamma Sal, why wouldn't she tell me if she was so hurt?" His chest tightened and released unsteadily, his panic about the upcoming conversation fading. "She didn't get a part she wanted?"

Mamma Sal sighed again. "Sweetie, this is part of her career. She auditions, and sometimes she gets it, sometimes she doesn't. In this case, she thought she had it nailed. It was a perfect part for her, right in her skill set, and they gave it to someone else. She'll be fine, I promise. I hate to say it, but

Rachel is used to this. They all are. This one just hurt a bit more."

David bit back the urge to swear and headed over to the flowers instead. "What do I need to do?"

"Nothing," Mamma Sal insisted. "If I know Rach, she already has another plan in place. Just go on with what you were going to do. Hug her a little longer if you must, but don't say anything. Now. Flowers?"

He wasn't happy with the forced change in topics, but he wasn't going to argue. "Her favorite. Please."

"Red and white roses, but let me tell you a secret. Ready?"

He smiled without effort, loving how Mamma Sal could do that to him. "Yeah."

"If *you* like the flowers, *she* will like the flowers. We're not that fidgety about it if the occasion isn't something significant. Just go with your gut, David. You'll be fine."

David found himself nodding, and, impossibly, relaxing. "Okay. You're the best, Mamma Sal."

"So are you, dear." She hung up before he could say anything else, leaving him to the collection of flowers before him.

He exhaled very slowly. Different colors and styles were all over the place, and, of course, there were no red *and* white roses. Red or white, nothing mixed, and no white roses with red tips just in case that had been what Mamma Sal meant. So he really was on his own.

No pressure.

"What do I like?" he murmured to himself, scanning the mass of flowers. He could honestly say he had never wondered what sort of flowers he liked before, and now seemed a terrible time to start. But all he really needed to know was if he liked something enough to give them to Rachel, right?

His eyes stopped on a bouquet of white, yellow, and purple flowers, the names of which did not exist in his brain.

But they reminded him of Rachel somehow. And they did have small white roses in them, so . . .

There were two versions of the bouquet, one that was cheaply wrapped and one that actually had full-sized roses as well, was in a vase, and had a white bow on the outside.

It was also way more expensive, not that it mattered.

Or did that matter?

Five minutes later, he was in his truck, roaring down the road, the vase of flowers buckled in, which looked ridiculous, but it worked. His dad's dog tags swung wildly from his rearview mirror, but David didn't care. He barely paid attention to it.

His mind spun instead on how he was going to say what he needed to say.

He couldn't lose Rachel.

He couldn't.

Her place was suddenly there before him, and he stared up at the balcony that was hers, feeling sick. What would this opportunity be if he lost her in the process? He'd been tossing everything over in his mind for days, and he couldn't keep it to himself any longer. The news would break soon, and she needed to be fully prepared for it when it did.

The same could be said for him.

Exhaling, he got out of the truck and grabbed the flowers and made his way up the stairs. Rachel knew he was coming over and knew they were going to talk, but he wished he had something else planned. Dinner or a movie or something. Anything.

Maybe she wouldn't want to do anything with him after this talk. She might need time. He knew she loved him; that had never been in question. But would that be enough for what lay before them?

Her door opened before he could knock, and his breath

caught at the sight of her. She wore an oversized red top and skinny black jeans, but her full lips curved in a gentle smile that made him feel like he was coming home.

"Hi," she said softly, her eyes flicking to the flowers. Her smile widened, and she looked back at him. "You apologizing or proposing?"

David laughed and leaned in to kiss her gently. "Cute. Can I come in?"

She pushed open the door, and he slid by her, kissing her again.

"I like this tradition," he murmured. "You do it with all your guests or just me?"

Rachel rolled her eyes. "Oh, everyone. I'm not particular."

"Generous." He held out the flowers without ceremony. "I didn't know what you'd like, but I thought . . ."

She took them, her smile gentling again. "I love them. Seriously, they are gorgeous." She inhaled them, sighing in satisfaction. "There is nothing like real flowers. And I can tell you didn't scrimp. Nicely done." She winked and set the vase on the counter, then surprised him by coming close and sliding her arms around his waist, hugging him tightly.

His arms encircled her out of pure instinct, and he laid his head against hers. "What's this? You okay?"

He felt her nod against him. "Perfect. I just wanted to hold you for a minute. And be held. You said we needed to talk, and that scares me."

"Hey." He rubbed his hands up and down her back slowly. "We do need to talk. But I love you, okay?"

"I know. I love you too." She pulled back and exhaled, her eyes on his. "So which team is getting you, babe?"

David's jaw dropped, and his hands fell to her hips. "How did you know?"

One corner of her mouth lifted in an almost smile, but there was a real sadness to her expression. "It wasn't hard to guess. So let's hear it."

He wet his lips, then admitted, "Chicago. The Flames."

Rachel's eyes widened, and then she grinned. "Are you *serious*? David!" She threw her arms around his neck, squealing. "Oh my gosh, you've got to be dying!"

"I am," he told her, somehow managing a weak smile. "I am, but . . ."

"But? What but?" She stepped back, eying him warily. "What?"

He moved past her and walked to the balcony, staring out at the night. "I knew this was a possibility when we were in Chicago, and I should have told you then, but . . . I didn't know how I felt about that possibility. I didn't want to say anything until it was real, and I still don't know."

"Are you kidding?" Rachel cried. "This is what you've always wanted, how do you not know?"

David turned and slid his hands into pockets, staring at her with all the pain currently turning in his stomach. "I don't want to leave you. Leave us. Leave this."

A furrow appeared on Rachel's brow. "Now you've got to be kidding."

"I'm not." He shrugged, swallowing hard.

Rachel was quiet for a moment, then began to close the distance between them. "Let me tell you something, David McCarthy. You don't get to worry over major things in this relationship without me. You don't make decisions about us without me, and you don't worry without me. Would you like to hear my thoughts on this whole thing?"

He nodded, unable to keep his eyes off of her, loving every inch of her and aching to sweep her into his arms again.

Rachel stood before him and folded her arms, "Are you

under the impression that this relationship only works in Pittsburgh? That for some reason it won't cross state lines? Because I didn't get that memo."

"Rach . . ."

She took his face in her hands. "I love you, David McCarthy. And I am willing to be with you no matter where you play, no matter where either of us live. I am Team Grizz, baby. And we're a national organization that you cannot shut down."

David kissed her before he could say anything that would ruin this incredible moment, and he kissed her hard. Cupping her face, he poured every ounce of relief and love into this connection, reaching for everything Rachel could offer him. Impossibly, he felt her reaching for him just as much.

He wasn't in this alone. He never had been. Rachel was in this too, and she was fighting for them.

For him.

"I love you, Rachel Bennett," he whispered against her lips, taking them one more time.

"Where's my ice cream, hot stuff?" she whispered back.

"In the truck."

"Let's take a walk and get it before it melts." She hummed and took his hand, leading him towards the door and slipping flip flops on. "Tell me about the contract."

David chuckled, shaking his head and gripping her hand. "They're buying out my arbitration and taking four years of my free agency, but they're offering six years, ten million a year, and a five-million-dollar signing bonus."

Rachel whirled, gaping at him, her eyes round. "Sixty-five million for six years? David!"

He fought a grin as they left the apartment. "In a few years, I won't be making as much as I could if I stuck it out and went free agent, but this . . ."

"This is worth it," she overrode. "This is a contender team, and it's stability on that team. Renegotiate when the contract is up, but take the offer."

Now he laughed. "I don't have much of a choice, you know. I'm basically bought and paid for."

Rachel nudged him hard, then looped her arm around his waist. "You would have chosen them anyway, and you know it."

"Yeah, that's true." He exhaled in the night air and pulled this incredible woman close. "And I choose us, babe. We'll figure this out, right?"

"Absolutely. Team Grachel, right?"

"You hate that name."

"But I love you, so let's come up with something better."

"Okay." He looked down at her, his mind whirling back to earlier and a certain phone conversation. "But first, how's the Andante stuff? You haven't said anything about it in a while. Things okay there?"

He felt Rachel stiffen just slightly, but she only shrugged. "Oh, sure. It's still there. Not much to say, honestly. Already started prep work for the next show." She looked up at him with a falsely bright smile. "Certainly nothing like your big news! Come on, you're only here another day before you're off to Michigan. Have you told your family about the trade yet?"

David frowned, but if she wasn't going to talk about it, he wouldn't force it.

He understood having secrets and not being ready to discuss them.

He only hoped she'd let him in on it whenever she was ready.

If she ever was.

Chapter 17

It had been a full week, and Rachel hadn't said anything further about Andante, about dance, or even about Chicago.

They were talking plenty and never seemed to run out of topics, but those three things were not part of any conversation. She was just as funny and engaging as she had ever been, and David doubted anyone but him and maybe her mom would have noticed anything was off. But she was definitely distracted, and she was a little clingier than normal.

He didn't mind that so much, he loved holding her any chance he got, but he couldn't deny that it was unusual. He'd had a few home games, and she'd come, but she had been late to each of them.

That wasn't a big deal; it just wasn't like her.

Rachel had let him tell his family about being traded to the Flames by himself, and she'd let him tell each member of the Six Pack. It was his news, she'd insisted, and she didn't want to steal any of his excitement about it.

He was pretty sure she hadn't even been the one to tell her mother, if Mamma Sal's reaction over the phone was to be believed.

Meghan had probably found out from Rachel, but he had no idea how that particular conversation had gone.

Everyone that knew was sworn to secrecy, of course. The exact details of the trade were still being worked out, and David had to finish this series against the Flames with the Knights before the news would break worldwide.

It was all such a blur to him still, so unreal. He was really going to move back to Chicago and play for his favorite team. He had a medical exam scheduled for while he was there, per protocol, but he knew there wouldn't be any hang-ups. He was as healthy now as he had ever been, and in way better shape than he had been in his Belltown days.

This was happening, and it was happening soon.

Maybe too soon.

It was a dumb thought; he knew the pace at which things moved in baseball, and he loved the rush of it all.

But he was in no rush to leave Rachel. Despite what she had said, he had more misgivings than he would admit. It wouldn't change a thing, wouldn't affect his move to Chicago, but being away from her on an almost-permanent basis would hurt. He didn't have the private jet that Big Dawg had, and the team's schedule was too insane to make any real plans for visiting. She wasn't wealthy, and her job at the dentist office only paid enough to take care of the bills.

They would be stuck between a rock and a hard place all too soon, and he was worried that once they discovered how hard this could be, one of them would give up.

He didn't want to think about that. He'd never been in a relationship like this one with Rachel, and he didn't want to try for another.

They *could* make this work.

They had to.

He hadn't asked her to come to Chicago with him, as

much as he wanted to. She had a life in Pittsburgh and a company to dance for. Her job wasn't much of an attraction, but her dancing was.

How could he ask her to give it all up for him?

The game last night in Chicago had been surreal, knowing this would soon be his home field. His family had taken him out for real Chicago pizza afterwards to celebrate, and it had been a blast. He would love being near them all again.

Today he was a little lost.

It was a three-game series with the Flames, so he was still in Chicago, and nothing was on his plate at the moment. Team warm-ups weren't for another few hours, and he'd already had a morning run to loosen himself up. He was due to meet up with Josie and Kate for milkshakes at their favorite place downtown, but he still had time before he needed to be there.

He wasn't exactly feeling the need to wander Chicago aimlessly, having seen most of it over the course of his life.

A buzzing in his pocket made him pause, and he reached for his phone, wondering which of the Six Pack or his brothers this would be.

His brows shot up as he checked the screen.

None of the above.

Meghan: 410 S Michigan Ave. 11:15. Trust me.

He stared at the message, then replied, *What?*

He waited for four heartbeats, but there was no sign of a response. Meghan was glued to her phone; she would have been quick, so this was an answer itself. Why was she texting him an address? She knew he was in Chicago, and . . .

She knew he was in Chicago. This was a Chicago address.

He hailed a cab and headed for the address, his head spinning. Why would he need to go here? What did he need to trust Meghan about?

A thought struck him, and he sat up straighter.

Rachel.

It didn't take long for the cab to reach the Fine Arts Center, as indicated by the sign outside of it, and he paid the fare, frowning up at the historic building.

What in the world could be going on in here?

He entered anyway and immediately saw a sign that read *Auditions* with an arrow. On a hunch, he followed, his mind spinning while his heart decided to skip to a beat he couldn't follow.

There was no way . . .

Carefully and quietly opening the auditorium door, David slipped in, checking his watch.

11:14.

Perfect.

David scooted sideways and leaned against the wall, keeping to the shadows of the mezzanine seats above him. He was fairly positive that he wasn't supposed to watch whatever auditions were taking place, but there wasn't exactly any security stopping him.

"Next?" a female voice called from a row of people sitting three or four rows from the stage.

It was only due to shock that he didn't actually gasp when he saw who came out onto the stage.

Rachel walked to the center of the stage, clothed in a black leotard and leggings, her hair slicked back. She met the eyes of the row for a moment, nodded, then crouched, wrapping her arms around her legs.

David's throat tightened in the silence, and he gripped the back of the chair in front of him.

The first strains of music began, and his heart began to ricochet off of his ribs. It was a slow, jazzy number that was familiar somehow, and Rachel seemed to bloom from the ground, her arms reaching first one direction, then the other before she spun loosely from the center of the stage.

She stopped, a hand going to her mouth, then her free arm extended before her to touch an invisible something. Her hand turned over, palm up, and then, somehow, she spun again as if a partner had turned her about.

The lyrics started as she began a series of moving jumps, always looking with joy at her invisible partner, and David's grip on the chair turned viselike.

It was the song from their night in Chicago together, the one they had danced to at the jazz restaurant.

Rachel suddenly became shy, skipping away and then turning around to gesture her partner towards her. She turned to face the audience, her eyes going heavenward. Her hands slid against her sides and wrapped around her front, exactly as they would have done if David had put his arms around her. Then she began to sway to the beat.

As if he were there behind her.

David had trouble swallowing as he watched her joyfully tumble to the ground and begin a series of turns and tumbling that perfectly displayed a giddy delight. She whirled on her knees, throwing her head back, arms flying out, arching backwards with inhuman flexibility before springing up again, this time to spin as perfectly and as fast as any ballet dancer he had ever seen.

Rachel turned again, this time her profile towards them, and she laid her head on some imaginary shoulder, her arms looping around the air as they would have around David's neck. She swayed to the beat four times, backing up with each sway, then dipped herself without the assistance of a partner. Straightening, she extended her leg, and David watched as, somehow, she created a cascade of ripples that coursed through her and that sent her springing around the stage with a height and stride that filled him with awe.

Returning to the center of the stage, Rachel swayed again,

her hands sliding across her body and up her neck until she stretched to her full length, going completely up on tiptoe. She arched backwards again and tumbled end over end, somehow making the motions graceful and elegant, even as athletic as they were.

She whirled, extended her hands forward, and turned in wide circles, clearly turning around and around with her partner. Just as the song came to its climax, she whirled out of the turns, and with a dramatic clasp of hands to her heart, grinning in full exhilaration, she dropped herself down to the ground, one hand staying on her heart, the other going to her brow like a swoon, her legs sprawling.

There was no sound for a full three heartbeats, and then the row of judges began to applaud.

Rachel sat up, smiling broadly, her chest heaving with panting breaths.

David was pretty sure he was doing the same thing, but he couldn't feel anything below his throat at the moment, and that was pretty painful.

"Thank you, Miss Bennett," the same woman from before said, sounding much warmer this time. "Such a beautiful, unique interpretation. We'll be in touch."

Rachel nodded and stood, running a hand through her still perfectly set blond hair.

David began to move towards the stage, though he wasn't sure how he could get to her without disrupting the audition process as a whole. He had no idea if that would affect her chances, but there was no way in hell he was leaving here without talking to her.

Or sweeping her into his arms and spinning her around until they were both sick.

She had managed to portray *them* up there. Without any assistance of lights or partners, she had captured their entire whirlwind, intense romance to the exact song that had given them their confessions of love.

Not only was Rachel an incredible artist, athlete, and dancer, but she had also given David a gift he felt wholly unworthy of.

The side curtain of the stage moved, and he saw Rachel jogging down the steps, now wearing a black jacket and carrying a small duffle over her shoulder. Her head was lowered, but she was smiling as she made her way up the aisle towards the exit, and him.

She ought to have been smiling. If she wasn't picked up for whatever company or production this was after that, there would be hell to pay, if David had any say in things.

He didn't, but still.

Rachel looked up as she neared him, and her smile faltered. She glanced back at the stage, then eyed David again. She exhaled heavily, and that gorgeous smile returned. She hefted her bag a little and continued towards him, her eyes trained on his.

"Baby," he whispered, shaking his head in disbelief.

She grinned in the full glory that was her natural essence and cupped his cheek. "That is what's important to me, babe. You and me. I'm not going to make you love me across state lines, though I know we could do it. I'm coming with you."

David covered her hand with his as her thumb stroked against his cheek.

"I know you would never ask me to leave my life in Pittsburgh," she went on, love shining from her eyes. "You wouldn't want me to give anything up. But I'm not giving anything up at all. Even if this audition fails, I can teach dance. You heard Sawyer, I'd be good at it, and I would love it. I could find another job too. I'm not worried about any of that; there are so many options for me. For us. All I really need is to be with you. I'm not giving you up. This is it."

"I love you," David whispered.

Rachel slid her hand around to the back of his neck, grinning smugly. "I love you too, Grizz McCarthy. Now kiss me good, and let's hunt for a place before you have to go to work."

David did kiss her, though whether it was good was up for debate.

He was of the opinion that it was extraordinary.

"Oh my gosh, I think I'm gonna cry."

"Mom . . ."

"Stop that, Clint. I can cry if I want to!"

"Mom, David is moving here. Why are you crying?"

Rachel laughed as Aubrey wiped at her eyes, handing her a tissue. "Moms cry, Clint . . ."

Clint gave her a dark look. "Thank you, Rachel. I had no idea."

"I am crying," Aubrey ground out while she dabbed the tissue at her eyes, "because this is the last time David will play at this field as a visitor. He goes back to Pittsburgh tomorrow, and then reports back up here on Tuesday. It's emotional!"

Rachel looked out at the field, her own emotions rising with an intensity. She hadn't thought about that. Of course she *had* thought about it, but not in depth.

They really were leaving Pittsburgh. They were coming here. She would be going to more games right here, sitting with the people beside her, and this would be home.

She looked around the historic park, inhaling the sights and sounds and smells of baseball. Then she looked back at the diamond, and, more particularly, at the man behind home plate.

The Knights' pitcher—she really couldn't remember who

their closer was tonight—came set, wound up, and threw, but a motion behind him caught her eye.

"Going!" she called, along with the entire McCarthy clan, jabbing a finger at the runner in the process of stealing third.

David caught the pitch and immediately sprang up, launching the ball over the head of the now-ducking batter in the direction of David Hansen, or Crocket, on third.

The ball got there just before the runner's foot tagged the base, and the umpire called him out.

Their little section roared in delight while the Flames fans around them groaned. The Knights players on the field cheered, and their bullpen began to dance in some bizarre choreographed horror that got a lot of attention.

Weirdos.

Rachel covered her cheeks as she grinned down at David. He'd thrown off his mask and helmet after the throw and was now whooping himself, patting his chest and pointing at Crocket. His polarized sunglasses, a much more sensible choice on the field than his traditional aviators, glinted in the sunlight as he removed those as well, wiping his face on his sleeve.

"That was *epic!*" Clint pumped a fist in the air. "Booyah, Grizzy!"

Almost as if he heard his brother, David looked up at them as he picked up his mask again. He grinned, and his eyes landed on Rachel. He touched his mouth and pointed those two fingers at her with a wink.

She nodded in response, one hand going to her heart.

David returned her nod, then turned back to face the pitcher, putting his mask on and going back down in position, punching his mitt twice.

The umpire leaned over, then suddenly scooted back, making the McCarthy brothers laugh as one.

"What?" Rachel demanded, looking down the line.

Tony took pity on her. "When an ump gets too close to Grizz's bubble, he drops a knee and scoots back just enough to cleat the guy a bit."

Rachel's jaw dropped. "And he doesn't get in trouble?"

All the McCarthy men shook their heads. "It's a complete accident," Tony assured her, using finger quotes for emphasis. "He apologizes profusely. Works every time."

She shook her head again and returned her attention to the game.

Two outs. Two strikes and one ball.

Almost there.

David was back to his usual position, and the Knights pitcher wound up, then threw a perfect strike to end the inning and the game. The crowd rose to their feet and applauded, cheering their beloved Flames in their victory over the Knights.

Rachel didn't care, and the McCarthys didn't care. They rose and cheered for their player, and Rachel moved down the line of cheering McCarthy family members.

How she knew, she had no idea, but she was ready when David pushed his mask up and turned to look for her. She grinned and waved as she continued down towards the dugout, weaving through some departing spectators. He matched her smile and removed his helmet entirely, dropping it to the ground.

This was it. This was the total romcom scene that no one would believe if they didn't see. This was exactly how the awkward doorstep waiting scene would pay off.

Meghan would die when she saw this on the news.

Tucking a strand of hair behind her ear, Rachel straightened her Team Grizz shirt proudly. She was only going to get one shot at this, and David had no idea it was coming.

They were starting to attract attention now, and the crowd was loving it. There were whoops, whistles, and hollers, and one intrepid woman bellowed, "Get it, girl!"

Rachel reached the bottom row of seats, taking advantage of the small space between the end of the net behind home plate and the railing separating the crowd from the dugout, where David was waiting. He laughed as she arrived, shaking his head and pushing his sunglasses on top of his head. "Subtle, Rach. Really subtle."

She shrugged and leaned towards him, the logistics of a baseball stadium making this a touch awkward. "I didn't want to leave any question marks. Much prefer to stake my claim."

He smirked and gave her a wink. "We probably should have met further down the third-base line. The stairs to the dugout are a barrier that makes this a lot less fun than it should be."

Rachel snorted a laugh and dropped her head. "There goes the romcom ending."

"The what now?"

"Never mind." She wet her lips and raised her head again, reaching out to stroke his beard a little. "We'll have plenty of time to get this scene right, babe. I'm not going anywhere."

He kissed the palm of her hand. "Neither am I."

Rachel let her hand go to his shoulder. "How does it feel? To play here knowing it's going to be your home base?"

David looked around and exhaled with satisfaction. "Like coming home."

"I'm so happy for you, babe." Rachel cupped his face with one hand. "We're going to do this. We are really doing this."

He smiled at her, nodding. "Yeah. We really are." He leaned in and kissed her, and she immediately opened for him, letting her lips play with his. She pressed further into him, straining to keep her balance against the barrier while she deepened the kiss between them.

Applause rippled around them and Rachel broke off, giggling to herself.

David chuckled and kissed her brow, his beard scratching against her skin. "Nicely done. That'll be all over the sports networks. Might even be a Top Ten play."

"It sure was." She wrinkled her nose and gave him another quick kiss. "Now how do you feel, David McCarthy?"

He brought a hand to her cheek and stroked it gently. "Like coming home."

Rachel smiled and sighed at the same time, feeling the now familiar swarm of butterflies that only David could make fly rise up in their delicious flurry. "Me too, babe. Me too."

Epilogue

"THAT LIFT WAS perfect, it was like we've been doing this together forever!"

"Right? And your *coupé* turns were spot on. Ballet background?"

"Not religiously, just a ballet bestie."

"Ah. I was ballroom myself. Well, it will be great to keep working with you, Rachel."

Rachel grinned at the tall, dark-haired guy with more charm than a purebred Italian man now strolling away from her. He was unquestionably the best partner she'd ever had in dance, and he had a fantastic sense of humor. She'd been with *Damhsa de Ghrásta* for a couple of weeks, and it had been exactly what she needed. Renewed passion for something she already loved, and she was eager for every minute of rehearsal.

For someone with a habit of hating rehearsal, it was a refreshing change.

The company was more like a large family than an organization, and there was such a variety of talents among them that Rachel felt like she was a kid stepping into the world's largest toy store. She just couldn't take everything in, and she wanted to spend ages to see everything.

Luckily, they had loved her audition and offered her a full position with the company. And they kept her plenty busy.

Rachel exhaled in satisfaction, slipping her hands into her jacket pockets. It had been a tough rehearsal, and she ached everywhere. Such a good ache, though.

She craned her neck and winced, then groaned when her phone rang. All she wanted was to soak in a hot bath and go to bed, not talk to people.

She glared at the screen of her phone, then laughed. "Hello, Megs."

"Girlfriend, I have discovered the roster for the Flames, and someone needs to call the fire department because this is *en fuego.*"

Rachel rolled her eyes and started the walk towards the metro. "Who did you find?"

"Ricky Palmer. Good. Gravy. And biscuits to go with it; I am in love." A clicking sound came through the phone. "Oh Lord, he is six foot four. Come to Mama, darling."

"Come visit me, and we'll talk," Rachel shot back. "Todd said he'd love another ballet specialist."

"Tell me I'm pretty too, and we'll arrange a rendezvous." Meghan laughed her usual raspy laugh. "How are things? Classes going okay?"

Rachel smiled at the thought. "So good. I knew I would enjoy dancing, but to have it actually be my job? Seriously, I may have to buy Todd a car out of sheer gratitude for absolutely making my life here in Chicago."

Meghan grunted once. "Shouldn't your hunk of burning love get your gratitude? I mean, *he* made your life there, right?"

"Hey."

Rachel looked up, and her jaw dropped.

David freaking McCarthy stood there in a leather jacket

next to a limo, aviators on, the lenses glinting in the light of sunset.

Her tongue went numb within her mouth, and her throat dried completely.

"Rach?" Meghan prodded.

"Yeah," Rachel responded through her completely parched lips. "Yeah, he made it." She hung up her phone and dropped it in her bag. "What in the world are you doing here? You're supposed to be in Kansas!"

David shrugged, grinning at her without shame. "We got rained out, so we've rescheduled for next month. The Stars needed to head out to LA, and I got the early flight home. I had to come celebrate the best dancer in Chicago."

Rachel hissed and made a face. "Sorry, Cady just left, and you missed her."

"Cady isn't the one who was mentioned as the dancer to watch in the *Chicago Arts and Entertainment* blog." David raised a brow and lowered his chin, staring more directly. "And she definitely isn't one of the Top Ten hottest dancers."

Rachel shivered but struck a casual pose. "I actually missed that issue of *Dancers Monthly.*"

"I saw it," David said in a low voice, pushing off of the limo and starting towards her. "Incredible photo spread. Stunning. Captivating. Breathtaking. Goddess-like and mind-blowing. And it didn't begin to do you justice."

Now her knees went weak, and another shiver raced up her spine. "Oof," she moaned, her eyes fluttering. "You are really getting on my good list, David McCarthy."

He leaned in and nuzzled against her, his lips just barely grazing hers before he pulled back, wincing. "Shame they only ranked you number five, though, I'd have put you higher."

Rachel barked a laugh and slapped his arm, then looped her arm around his neck and pulled him in for a kiss that ought to have made them both senseless.

Anytime they laughed while kissing drove them wild, and it was the best time.

Out in the Chicago evening, though, it wasn't quite the same.

David broke off and hummed in satisfaction, pulling her in for a tight hug. "I missed you, babe. How was rehearsal?"

Rachel kissed his neck and rested her head against his shoulder. "Great. I love being this sore. And this is such a good group, David. I love it."

"I can tell." He smiled down at her. "You're glowing, and that makes me happy. Classes okay?"

Rachel nodded again as David led her to the limo. "The little girls are learning so fast, and my advanced group? They are so much better than I was at their age." She narrowed her eyes as she peered at him. "Where are you sweeping me off to?"

David leaned in and kissed her again. "Wherever you want, my love. We are celebrating you. I'll go anywhere."

She patted his cheek, then gripped his beard and tugged playfully. "Pancakes, David McCarthy. Pancakes for dinner with my man sounds fabulous."

A spark lit in his eyes, and he nodded. "Absolutely." His phone buzzed, and he made a face as he pulled it up. Then he snorted. "Oh boy. Axe Man lost tonight and they lost bad. He had a whopper of a bad play, and the boys are wringing him out." He showed her the text thread, chuckling.

Rachel laughed, shaking her head. "You guys . . . Okay, time to distract them from him. We're sending them all a video when we get our pancakes. You know how Ryker feels about pancakes, and Cole hates being left out of anything, so . . ."

David kissed her suddenly, and it was as fierce as it was brief. "I love you so much," he laughed as he opened the door for her.

Rachel quirked her brows and slid into the limo. "Love you too, babe. Now tell me about Kansas. Who'd you have to room with this time?"

He slid in next to her and took her hand, their fingers automatically lacing, and as they headed out to get pancakes, David told her all about the ill-fated trip to Kansas and had her cracking up in no time.

The next game was in three days, and it was at home in Chicago, but there would be a surprise for Grizz McCarthy at that game. An entire fan section for Team Grizz with matching shirts and hats, and some very boisterous Belltown cheers that would get the crowd going.

Team Grizz was in full force in Chicago, and she was the captain of that team.

She grinned at him in the limo, knowing he would both hate and love what they had planned. The Six Pack were in on it, and they would chime in with their pictures after their games. None of their shirts said Team Grizz, and they refused to tell Rachel what they said, but it would be worth it.

"I love you, you know," she murmured, feeling a surge of tenderness.

David looked at her, then kissed the hand he held, his eyes staying on hers. "Yeah, baby, I know. And I'm a hundred and fifty percent positive I love you back. Always will."

"Hmm," Rachel mused, "that does sound serious."

He pulled her in and kissed her brow. "Anything over a hundred is forever. Hope you're ready."

Rachel leaned back and narrowed her eyes at him. "Are you going to propose to me over pancakes?"

"No." David scoffed and shook his head. "Everybody knows you don't propose or apologize without flowers."

"So any time you give me flowers, I should be suspicious?" she shot back. "Sometimes we like flowers for no reason, you know."

He grinned playfully. "I know. After shows, to make you smile, to break big news, to show you I love you . . . You'll get plenty of flowers."

Dang, she loved it when he was flirtatious and playful. She leaned into him and rested her chin on his chest, still looking up at him. "You're going to leave me on the edge of my seat? I should always anticipate a proposal and just wait in hopes that you actually do it someday?"

He gave her a long, slow kiss that curled her toes. "*When* I propose to you, Rachel Bennett, I will leave no doubt. Believe me, you will know."

Rachel smiled dreamily at this man she loved so much. "I'm a hundred and fifty-one percent sure I will say yes."

David kissed her again, very softly. "Good."

She nuzzled up against him with a sigh, drawing his arm around her like a blanket. "So help me, David McCarthy, if you propose to me over a jumbotron at a baseball game, I will say no until you do it right."

He coughed a laugh, his arm tightening around her. "Noted, babe. No jumbotron."

"In fact, don't do anything that will get the media's attention."

"Can't promise that one. Six Pack rules the media, so . . ."

"You're planning a public proposal?"

"Team Grizz will want to know. It's only fair we share it with them."

"If you get Cole's dad to land the helicopter in the outfield during the seventh inning stretch, so help me . . ."

"Well, there goes that idea." He pulled out his phone and pretended to make a call. "Cancel the helicopter, Dawg. Back to the drawing board."

Rachel snorted a laugh and buried her face into his chest. "Don't ask my pretend boyfriend how my real boyfriend should propose. You figure it out. I'll marry *you*, not him."

"Is that a yes?" David teased, tipping her face up to his.

She smiled and quirked her brows. "Ask me the right way, and we'll see," she murmured, arching up to kiss him one more time.

Just because.

Acknowledgments

This book would not have happened without some very important people.

Shout out to Bob for being my catcher guru and explaining minute details to me.

Shout out to Hannah and Alicia for all the dancing terminology, choreography ideas, and endless corrections.

And, as always, shout out to my big brother, the baseball nerd. Couldn't have done it without our random yet oddly specific baseball themed text conversations. Thanks a million, Chris! Take me out to the ballgame, okay?

Rebecca Connolly writes romances, both period and contemporary, because she absolutely loves a good love story. She has been creating stories since childhood, and there are home videos to prove it! She started writing them down in elementary school and has never looked back. She currently lives in Indiana, spends every spare moment away from her day job absorbed in her writing, and is a hot cocoa addict.

Visit her online: RebeccaConnolly.com